The Mr. & Mrs. Club

by

Alan Emmet

THE PERMANENT PRESS
SAG HARBOR, NY 11963

Library of Congress Cataloging-in-Publication Data

Emmet, Alan
    The Mr. & Mrs. Club: a novel / by Alan Emmet
      p. cm.
    ISBN 1-57962-032-9 (alk. paper)
    1. Married women--Fiction. 2. Massachusetts--Fiction.
    3. Young women--Fiction. I. Fiction.

    PS3555.M429 M7 2001
    813'.6--dc21   00-064271
                                    CIP

This is a ficitonal work. The characters and incidents in the novel are invented.

THE PERMANENT PRESS
4170 Noyac Road
Sag Harbor, NY 11963

For Woods

Hello Loneliness

THE JUICE from the strawberries made Liza's fingers look wounded. She was getting the knack of hulling, picking one berry after another from the basket beside her, and flicking off the leafy hulls with her sharp little knife. Green stars fell onto the newspaper at her feet. Shiny red berries dropped into a battered gray saucepan.

"You ain't nothing but a . . ." her hips moved . . . "houn' dog."

She'd brought the radio out to the screen porch and plugged it in. Since there was nobody around, she could play whatever she wanted. It was Tuesday, so Julius was at a school committee meeting. Abby was asleep in her crib upstairs.

Elvis Presley was supposed to be shocking, moving his hips so provocatively, and making love to his guitar. No one Liza knew even bothered to talk about him. Still, she'd seen the headlines, heard women cluck over him as they wheeled their grocery carts around the Atomic Super Market. But the music was in Liza, her feet, her hips, her shoulders. She let each strawberry drop in time with the beat.

"Cryin' all the time . . ."

The announcer's voice was smooth, like some silky cream you might rub into your skin. As he talked about the music, he promised more. You could hear the lick of his tongue as he touted the "suc-culent veal parmigiana," the "umm-luscious linguine alfredo," at a certain Charlestown restaurant. He lingered over the words ". . . sin-fully rich desserts . . ." as if he were right there beside her.

"Bye-bye, happiness; hello, loneliness . . ." The melliflous Everly brothers. Liza paused over a strawberry, thought of other people, other times, other places. Already it seemed so long ago.

"I think I'm a-gonna cry-y." The voice shook in time with the words. Liza moved her hands with the beat. A drop fell into the berries, then another; tears. Liza pushed at her eyes with red fingers, almost truly wounding herself with the knife.

When she heard the scrunch of tires on the gravel, she snapped off the radio. Julius's big shoes came clumping up the steps and into the room. "How can you see what you're doing?" he said. "It's dark! You could turn on a light." He did. "You've got red all over your face."

Liza looked up to see his frown. "I'm just about finished," she said. "I think I have enough to freeze."

This was the beginning of Julius and Liza Prescotts' second summer in their old farmhouse. It was a year to the day since they'd moved in. Liza remembered sitting on the granite doorstep in the sun, five-month-old Abby crawling through the uncut grass, while they waited for the moving van to get there from Cambridge, bringing all the stuff from their apartment. The air was scented with lilies-of-the-valley.

Abby was born just after midnight on New Year's Day, 1955. The timing seemed exciting and significant to Liza. Hers might be the first baby in the whole world to be born in 1955. Liza could remember every single thing about that evening. Bert and Selena, their best law-school friends, had come over. Bert opened the champagne early, when Liza began having pains. Julius had gone first down to the car, carrying the suitcase Liza had packed weeks before: the pink trousseau bed-jacket she'd never worn, a tiny white nightgown for the baby, and lily-of-the-valley cologne and talcum for herself. She carried a glass with her as she trundled heavily down the outside stairs from their second-floor apartment.

"Good-bye! Good-bye . . ." They all waved. None of them knew anything about babies. Having babies was something that came with being married, like ironing your husband's shirts.

"Wish me luck, you guys," Liza called over her shoulder.

She still remembered the closing of the hospital elevator door, slowly cutting off her view of tall, pale, cool, unsmiling Julius, shutting her in with the nurse and the suitcase, sending her up to who knew what. That clear vision of Julius stayed with her, long after she was back home again — living with him, talking to him, sleeping every night in the same bed with him. The man she had looked at from the closing door of the hospital elevator was someone she didn't really know.

The English Major's Future

THE FIRST TIME Liza had seen Julius, he was zooming down the steepest trail at Cranmore, all in black like the ski instructors. In what still seemed to Liza her boldest move ever, she managed, by dallying at the base of the lift, to sit beside Julius on his next trip up the mountain. She loved the lift at Cranmore, the "Ski Mobile," because you could ride two and two. *And* because it went on a track like a little train, so you didn't have to dangle over the tree tops. "Good for people like me, with height phobia," she told Julius as they rolled slowly up the mountain.

That got his attention. "Well, really." He looked at her. "So what do you think you're doing on skis? It's all about heights."

"I know." She leaned her forehead into her mitten. "I could never keep up with you in a million years."

It turned out that they were both at college in Cambridge. Julius was a senior, Liza a sophomore. Back there again, after their semester break, Liza had registered for a medieval history course he was taking, hoping he'd notice her on his way out. Bored by the lectures, Liza would inscribe in a corner of her notebook, in miniscule script, all the qualities that summed up Julius for her:

>Smart (later changed to Brilliant)
>Handsome
>Suave (she'd crossed out Smooth)
>Well-read
>Well-dressed
>Dashing
>Polite
>Sense of Humor (he was so perfect that Liza was sure he must have one.)

Late at night, in pajamas and red quilted robe, Liza scrunched down in a wicker chair in a corner of the third-floor smoking room in Bertram Hall, listening to the graduating seniors talking about their futures. The smoke had made a cloud layer so thick that when you stood up you could hardly see. Jo Dorfman had heard that day that she'd landed a job in Washington at the CIA, very hush-hush. That's what *I* wanted to do, Liza thought. Just last fall she used to picture herself in high heels and a swirly dress, big sunglasses and a scarf wrapped over her hair, maybe a tiny little Derringer in her purse, as she headed off on a secret mission, perhaps a rendezvous in the bar of the Hotel Metropole. But now it was spring, and to her surprise she didn't envy Jo at all.

Sonya Hurwitz, in a black wrapper with her hair falling over one eye, was jubilant. "So who says there's no future for English majors?" She was going to work at *Life* magazine.

Daphne Cole was also headed for New York, to a job at Alfred A. Knopf. "Yeah, I guess *Beowulf* was worth it after all."

Liza watched her light another Lucky from the one she had. Daphne's hair was flattened into a maze of concentric circles, each curl spiked with a bobby pin. Liza couldn't picture her in some publisher's carpeted office. That's what I *really* wanted to do, Liza told herself, something literary, crossing my nyloned legs at a desk in the city room, conferring with reporters and editors in green eyeshades, smoking, typing fast and badly, going out on assignment. Now all that had lost its glamour, too. Lately her only image of her future self was at the wheel of a wood-paneled station wagon filled with blond kids — two, four, six — and a big black dog.

She'd been seeing a lot of Julius that spring. He'd wanted to have her with him, that was obvious. He swept her up in a whirlwind of lunches in the Square, foreign movies, crew races, and parties with his friends, who all laughed a lot. Serious Julius frowned and talked. Why didn't I flunk out? she wondered afterward; I practically stopped doing any work at all.

Julius was cramming for his Law Boards and writing his thesis, which took a lot of time— something about Thomas Aquinas, very complicated.

"I don't think I can see you for a couple of weeks," he told her on the phone one night. "I've gotta get this done."

Liza had offered to help, and then did. She arranged file cards in stacks all up and down the stained gray carpet of his room in Eliot House. Hunched over her own Smith Corona, she typed his bibliography. When at last he was ready to turn in the hefty final product, she climbed with him up three flights of wooden stairs to the history department office in Boylston Hall. After that, he sank exhausted into a booth at Cronin's. He took a long first swig of Carling's Black Label, then reached across the table for Liza's hand. "I couldn't have done it without you," he said.

Liza felt her face grow warm. This is the best moment of my entire life, she'd thought.

A year later, they were married. Two years after that, in the spring of 1955, when Abby was five months old, they'd bought this house in the country. Liza remembered how even before they moved in, she'd thought how romantic it was to move to an old house on a winding road, with fields and woods around it, and the shaggy remains of a garden. Paint was flaking from the house, outside and in, but Liza could hardly wait to pick out colors and wallpapers, make curtains out of flowered sheets the way the *Ladies' Home Journal* advised. Neither she nor Julius had known one thing about frayed wiring, dripping faucets, leaky tanks, rotting floorboards. They still didn't. But, as she'd told their friends, they had *four* fireplaces! Julius would stomp out to the woods on Sunday morning with his Swedish saw to cut firewood, while Liza, alone again with Abby, stroked pink Chem Tone onto the walls of their bathroom and listened to the radio.

It took Julius two hours each day to commute to his new job at the very best law firm in Boston. He had bought a second car right after they moved, a little white Henry J, so Liza could have the station wagon to go shopping or take Abby for her check-ups.

"The Henry J's the cheapest car on the market," he'd boasted. Pieces started to drop off right away, little things like the rear-view mirror, a window crank, the handle of the emergency brake.

Liza and Julius didn't think of their old house as belonging to any town, really, although of course it did. Rock Hill looked rural. The town center was postcard-perfect, with two white-steepled churches facing each other across a triangular green common. Apple trees patterned the slopes behind crumbling stone walls that bordered narrow winding roads.

It was hard to get to know anybody in Rock Hill. The houses on their road were scattered, separated by fields. Some of the houses hadn't been painted in so long that their clapboards were stark, bare, and gray. Most of the people looked older, and — well — different: stout men in caps and bib overalls, and lean women in bib aprons, their faces weathered to the bone like the houses. But Julius would read the weekly paper. "Hmm," he'd say when he found something that interested him. Liza heard him calling up people, with the paper folded to a certain page. Before she knew it he'd signed up for a town committee to talk about moving the dump. He got on the building committee at church, and decided to run for the town school committee. He was sure he'd win. Liza was sure he wouldn't. When he won, Liza decided that in such a small town almost anyone who wanted to could probably get elected to the school committee. Naturally, she knew better than to say that. She just smiled her Mona Lisa smile, and told Julius how proud she was.

Standing over the suds-filled sink one morning, absently scouring the pots from dinner the night before, Liza thought about Julius. He really hasn't changed at all in the four years since I first met him, she decided, and I'm still not sure he has a sense of humor. Running more hot water, she looked at her reddened hands, fingers fanned out, wrinkled from long immersion. At least my nails are clean, she thought.

The Buzzing of Bees

ONE STILL September day, Selena drove out for a long-planned visit to see Liza. Molly, another of Liza's Cambridge friends, came with Selena and their two little children. Months before, when Julius and Liza were still trying to decide whether to buy the house, Selena had spotted the old apple trees behind it. "Think of all the pies we can make!" she'd crowed. Maybe that had been the deciding factor.

Now the apples were red and ripe, small hard crabapples, fit for jelly rather than pies. A canvas bag dangled from Molly's shoulder; Selena and Liza carried baskets. The children played in the long grass while their mothers picked. Liza's tree was full of bees, buzzing in the warm sun. Selena's and Molly's voices sounded shrill. They worked their way around the trees, filling their baskets with wine-dark fruit. "Watch out for the bees," Selena cried.

Liza polished a queer little apple in her hand; it was shaped like a baby's bottom.

"It doesn't matter if they're not perfect," Molly called. "We're going to have so much jelly!"

Before long, Abby got stung. Her eyes opened in surprise, then her face crumpled, and she turned toward Liza, screaming, with her hands over her ears. Liza swept her up, hugging, patting, feeling guilty.

"Don't you ever get lonely out here?" asked Selena, as they ate their sandwiches. She and Molly leaned back in the two green Adirondack chairs; Liza perched on a chair she'd brought out from the kitchen.

"Well, there's a lot to do." Liza didn't answer the question. "More curtains to make. I'd like to try wallpapering

Abby's room. Maybe jam from all the wild grapes. And I want to make a flower garden. I never have enough time, it seems."

"Your house has plenty of room for a big family . . ."

Liza thought about that. She listened to the insect sounds — the humming, the buzzing — and the voices of her friends. She poured more iced tea.

Molly and Selena were talking about where they would live, where their husbands might practice — and how many babies they might have. Selena's husband came from a big family; the wives of his older brothers were having babies just about every year.

Liza got a sinking feeling just thinking about having five children, or six. I'm not strong enough, bold enough, old enough, she thought, and besides, trying to be a perfect mother to Abby takes most of the day already. But lots of people seemed to do it all — people she knew about, like Julius's cousins. Those mothers, with their kids, their dogs, their station wagons, blonde and tan at the beach in two-piece bathing suits, not a care in the world, it seemed. Liza pulled the limp mint out of her tea and ate it. She sat up straight, wondering if Julius expected her to be just like those cousins.

"How many kids do you think you'll have, Molly?" Liza asked.

"Oh, we might stop at four." Molly sounded dreamy. She yawned.

Four. Liza brushed a bee off the rim of her glass, and took a long sip.

Frozen Food

YOU HAD to have a deep freeze if you lived in the country. Liza and Julius got a big one at Sears. Not the largest, but still — a chest, rather than an upright.

"I can use the top of it for folding laundry," Liza said. When the men delivered the freezer, it wouldn't fit through the door. They had to take out a window to get it in, but there was room for it at the end of the kitchen, right next to the washing machine with the porthole window.

"Abby thinks she's watching television when the clothes go round." That's what Liza liked to tell their Cambridge friends. They were so smug, all of them, including Julius, about not having TV.

Julius worked in the vegetable garden on Saturday mornings. Their best crop the first year was New Zealand spinach. Liza didn't like it very much, no matter how she cooked it. It was not at all like real spinach, but of course she didn't say anything. New Zealand spinach was good because it kept growing no matter how hot it got. And it was hot that summer. They had so much New Zealand spinach that Liza froze some for next winter.

The kitchen filled up with steam while Liza boiled water to blanch the so-called spinach. She let Abby play with the cans of Campbell's soup, anything to keep her at the far end of the kitchen, out of harm's way. A few of the labels got pulled off, so later sometimes Liza wouldn't know whether it would be tomato soup for lunch, or cream of celery.

She liked filling the new freezer with little blue freezer boxes. She kept them separate from the Bird's Eye vegetables she bought at the Atomic Super Market. It was good to have things like that on hand. Just in case.

15

One of Julius's friends at the law firm talked him into going halves on a frozen steer.

"It's much cheaper that way," Julius told Liza. "And then you have it. Brad says it's really good beef, too. Tender. We're lucky he's letting us share."

They drove over to Brad's house one Saturday to pick up their share. It looked to Liza like a lot of meat. Too much for their freezer. But they'd already rented a locker where they could store the extra meat.

One sweltering July day, when supplies were getting low in their home freezer, Liza took Abby in the station wagon to the Rock Village Frozen Storage place on the other side of town. Behind the wooden counter huge white carcasses dangled from metal hooks. The butchers wore white aprons smeared with blood.

Why don't they give them red aprons? Liza wondered. Or brown.

"Locker thirty-eight," she told the man.

He gestured toward the big door. "We'll keep the baby, if you want. Real cold in there."

But Liza had brought Abby's blue snowsuit jacket, along with a special metal basket in which to carry the meat.

When she pulled open the thick, heavy door to the storage room, steam came billowing out. The door clanged shut behind them as she dashed right to their locker.

Clutching Abby in one arm, she filled the metal basket with hard, slippery, white-wrapped packages, not bothering to read what parts of the meat she was taking. She tried to grab a few big packets, along with the little ones of hamburger or liver. A heavy rump roast fell on Liza's foot. She was wearing sandals, and her toes were bare.

"Hold on tight," she said to Abby. Liza imagined herself on one of those polar expeditions her mother used to read about while she was slowly dying. Hugging Abby and the basket to her, Liza ran limping toward the big door. She couldn't remember whether she'd have to unlatch the door, or pound on it. Out of breath, she fell against the door. How much time before we freeze to death? Abby started crying. "Please! Let us out," Liza called, banging with her fist. When the door opened, steam surged out with them. Liza's glasses fogged up, and for a minute she couldn't see. She heard the butchers laughing.

By the time she drove into their driveway, Liza felt wilted from the heat, her blouse sticking to the back of the seat.

When Julius got home from the office, Liza had already tucked Abby in bed and changed into her pink-striped Lanz dress, the one with the shell buttons. She had dinner all ready to take out to the porch: cold curry soup and chicken salad, summer recipes she'd torn out of a magazine. She held her arms out to Julius.

"No, no, no. Please." He shrank back from her. "It's much too hot."

Leaves From the Family Tree

EVERY SINGLE household task brought Liza's mother back to her. As she tore a frayed blue Oxford shirt of Julius's into clean rags, Liza could picture her mother at her sewing machine, painstakingly pulling out the tiny stitches from one of Liza's father's white shirts, then turning the collar and re-stitching it so that the frayed part was out of sight. "Remember this for life, Liza. Now this shirt will be good for another two years, maybe three." Liza, perhaps thirteen at the time, could hardly have cared less. But she remembered.

There were so many lessons like that, most of them aimed at avoiding waste and saving money. She'd only just learned that the proverbial "stitch in time" that supposedly saved nine was not a saying invented by her mother. Liza would feel a spasm of guilt when she neglected to make chicken soup out of the gnawed bones from last night's dinner, or let Abby have her lime jello before she'd eaten all her peas. Liza, in her own kitchen, could hear her mother's voice and her edicts, gentle but firm: "Always use the whisk so you won't have lumps in your cream sauce."

Well, but she missed her mother, too. Those strictures were somehow comforting. They made a whole skeleton to hang your life on. You knew the rules; if you simply followed them you'd always know where you were, and everything would just . . . work out.

The only trouble was, everything hadn't worked out so well for her mother, in the end. When Liza had come home for Christmas during her sophomore year at college, her mother was puzzled that her feet felt numb. Her feet sometimes refused to do what she told them. Dr. Ackerly, the best doctor in Dilworth, Pennsylvania, their family doctor forever, had found nothing wrong.

"Psycho-somatic," Liza's Aunt Abigail hissed in Liza's ear. But neither Liza nor her father believed that the mother and wife who so dominated their lives could possibly be subject to any *mental* failing. Nevertheless, they and Dr. Ackerly acceded gratefully to Aunt Abigail's proposal to accompany Liza's mother to the Mayo Clinic for a thorough "work-up."

Aunt Abigail and Liza's mother had a high old time at the Mayo. "Oh, that neurologist," Aunt Abigail said, smiling and shaking her head. "He was the best-looking thing . . . *exactly* like Douglas Fairbanks."

"All the doctors are *so* bright, so young, and *so* interested in me," said Liza's mother. "And my nurses were absolutely adorable. We just laughed and laughed, didn't we, Abigail?"

You'd think they'd been on a cruise, thought Liza. But when all the reports came back, it turned out that the Mayo Clinic hadn't found anything wrong, either.

Still Liza's mother had grown steadily worse. She began walking with a cane. She complained that it hurt her to stand. Mostly, now, she just sat in her favorite armchair, reading accounts of polar expeditions, or attempts at climbing Annapurna and the north face of the Eiger. When she was home for Thanksgiving, Liza observed from behind her own book that her mother's pages seldom turned. Her father had taken over the shopping and errands. Her mother's only outings seemed to be the weekly appointments with Mario the hairdresser, who'd curled and coiffed her mother for as long as Liza could remember.

Liza dreaded coming home, dreaded the evidence of continuing decline. When she and Julius Prescott were engaged, just before Christmas, Liza hardly dared tell her parents, fearing that a wedding would throw her mother into a panic or worse. "We just want a simple, tiny wedding. You won't need to do a thing, Mummy," Liza said.

But both her parents were thrilled. They thought Julius

was perfect. "So good-looking. And such lovely manners," said her mother.

"He has a good head on his shoulders," said her father, who also gathered that Julius would be able to provide for Liza in something more than the plain, suburban style to which, as the daughter of a vice-president of the local bank, she was accustomed.

Liza's mother perked up. She became like her old self. In letters to Liza, back at college in Cambridge, she'd write, "During the January thaw, Daddy drove me over to McCutcheon's for their white sale. I ordered a dozen percale sheets and pillowcases for you, seconds, but not so as you'd notice. Now about towels. Miss Eileen is holding the blue ones for me, and also a nice soft shade of green if you'd rather. We must let her know, so telephone me as soon as you get this (after 5:00, of course)."

During spring break, Liza and her mother went to Dayton's to buy clothes for Liza's trousseau. If Liza couldn't decide between two embroidered nightgowns or two jewel-colored silk dresses, Liza's mother — who'd always prided herself on being so "Scotch," always looking out for a bargain — would say, with a blissful smile, "Get them both, dearie."

Miss Rose the dressmaker was altering Liza's mother's wedding gown, so maybe that was a saving, thought Liza. She was the one who worried about money now, fearful that they were spending far more than her father's salary at the Dilworth Trust Company would allow.

The sun shone on the wedding. Looking at herself in the mirror before the ceremony, Liza felt beautiful. Her grey-haired father, straight and lean, walked her up the aisle behind the flower girls, Julius's twin nieces. Liza gasped when she saw Julius, so tall and handsome, with a blue bachelor's button in his lapel. Liza's mother, in a long pearl gray gown, a feathered cap, and flowers on her cane, sat in the front pew, looking smaller than she used to, but beaming happily. Turning on Julius's arm after the ceremony, Liza blew a kiss toward her mother. She felt then a sharp tug from Julius, reminding her to stand up straight and walk down the aisle with him, the virgin bride.

The reception was at Aunt Lolly's and Uncle Ferd's, the old many-gabled house where Liza's father and Uncle Ferd had grown up, much grander than Liza's parents' modest Dutch Colonial. Everyone tried to make Liza's mother stay sitting in an armchair in the middle of the tent, but she kept hopping up on her cane, laughing and greeting people, saying she wanted to dance with the groom.

Julius's father made one of his rare appearances at the wedding, a shadowy, gray figure who stayed quietly in the background. He found himself a chair in a corner of the tent. Whenever one of Liza's aunts approached him, he'd make a feint at standing, until they'd say, "No, no, please don't get up. I just wanted to say hello to the father of the groom." Then they'd scurry away. The few times she'd met Mr. Prescott, with his unfocused eyes, his hoarse voice, and his cryptic comments, Liza had found him scary. It didn't help when she learned that he was always slightly drunk. At college she'd known boys who got drunk, but they were loud. Julius, of course, was used to his father, but still, as he told Liza later, he'd kept hoping that he wouldn't fall down at their wedding. Julius's mother, Minx, had left his father for good about the time that Julius went off to boarding school. Since then, his father had lived at his club in New York, theoretically managing his stock portfolio, but more likely, in Julius's opinion, slowly drinking himself to death.

Minx, who had married Gubby on an impulse soon after her Nevada divorce came through, was still married to him at the time of Julius's and Liza's wedding. But Minx laughed at Gubby, both to his face and behind his back. She had her eye out for greener fields. In her tight dress — shocking pink with a slit up one side — and the highest heels anyone in Dilworth had ever seen on a real person,

Minx outshone all Liza's bridesmaids. Julius admitted to Liza on their honeymoon that he'd half expected her to latch embarrassingly onto one of Liza's uncles or old family friends at the wedding.

Liza was an only child, but Julius had an older sister, Vanessa, who was of course a bridesmaid even though Liza had never laid eyes on her before the wedding. She lived way out in Hollywood, the real Hollywood. Her husband Lionel was English and supposedly involved in films. No one said exactly what it was he did. For the wedding he wore a white suit and two-toned brown and white shoes with little perforations all over them. Both Lionel and Vanessa were unusually blond and unusually tan, even though it was only June. Their twin flower girl daughters were blonde, too. "Olivia! Alicia!" Vanessa's piercing soprano rang through the tent at intervals, temporarily drowning out the strolling accordion. "Alicia! Olivia!" Liza saw them eating the yellow sugar roses off the cake before she'd even cut it.

Meanwhile, Gubby, resplendent in double-breasted pinstripes, a puffed-out red dotted tie, and gold cufflinks the size of walnuts, caused a little flurry of his own. He'd arranged with the elderly bellman at the Hotel Dilworth, where the out-of-towners were staying, to bring two large cartons to the wedding reception. Gubby was all in a twitter as he paid off the bellman and opened up the boxes. Carrying on a monologue with himself and whoever was nearby, he unpacked a dozen or more identical bottles.

"What is it?" someone asked.

"Perfume!" said a bridesmaid.

"Too bad it's not Jack Daniel's," said an usher.

Ignoring all comments, Gubby tottered on pointy black shoes to Liza, first, then to her mother, and in turn to each of Liza's bridemaids and her aunts. To each one he offered, with a neat bow, a bottle of Arpège perfume. They looked like display bottles in the store, Liza thought, the ones that nobody ever buys.

"It's as big as a milk bottle!" laughed Liza's mother. Liza kissed Gubby on the ear. "Thank you," she said. "Just think, now we'll all smell alike," said Aunt Abigail.

"Oh, *Gubby*," Minx said, rolling her head back.

By the end of the day Liza's cheeks hurt from smiling. As she and Julius set off on a honeymoon cruise to Bermuda, Liza was elated that the two sides had seemed to get on so well at their wedding, her relatives — so ordinary, in her fond opinion — and Julius's family, so thrillingly glamorous.

"I wouldn't be surprised if we cured your mother," Julius said, lifting his glass of champagne.

"*Maybe.*" Liza was not convinced. "Anyhow, I think she had more fun on our wedding day than ever in her whole life."

A year later Liza's mother was dead, thus proving, at least, that her illness was not just in her mind. Weeping in Aunt Abigail's arms after the funeral, Liza sobbed, "I never had a chance to tell her I'm pregnant."

Hearts

IT WAS a mystery to Liza where Julius's lively social conscience had sprung from. Maybe from one of those eminent grandfathers who'd made money, and then donated a new wing to the Home for Incurables, or a gym to Bethany Bible College. But anyhow, Julius cared in his way about the poor and downtrodden, applauded the Supreme Court's decision in *Brown v. Board of Education*, served on the school committee in Rock Hill (where no one had ever seen a person of any distinguishing color), and now, on the basis of a phone call, had agreed to canvas their neighborhood for the Heart Fund.

"It'll be a good chance to meet people," he told Liza. "Sunday afternoon they'll probably all be home. I'll walk."

He decided to wear his suit. "So it won't look as if I'm dressing down," he told her. He put the fliers in his briefcase, along with the little red cardboard hearts he was supposed to give people even if they didn't contribute.

He was gone for almost two hours. Liza happened to be looking out the window when he walked up the driveway. He didn't look quite as . . . upright as usual. Liza thought he might not have wanted her to see him just then looking as if he might have failed.

"How did it go?" she asked brightly when he came into the kitchen.

Julius let his briefcase drop. He opened the refrigerator and peered in. "Isn't there any beer?" One, thank goodness. Liza poured it into a glass the way he had taught her, so it didn't suds over.

Later, over dinner, he told her about it.

"Mrs. Cormier wasn't home. That black dog of hers didn't even move off the doormat; just thumped its tail. At least it's friendly. The next house was really weird, you know, the one with no paint? It's hard to tell around here which door you're supposed to go to. No one seems to use their front door."

"Well, we don't either . . . much," Liza said. She was studying her broken fingernails, her engagement ring.

"Liza, you don't understand. We have a good path; it's obvious which door people should use. But these people around here . . . do you want to hear this or not?"

"Of course I do! I'm fascinated." Liza sat up very straight. She held her fork in mid-air so it would look as if she were spellbound.

"The only car at that house was up on blocks, so I didn't know if anyone was home. But when I knocked at the screen door, I could hear a chair scrape on the floor. So I waited, and pretty soon this old guy came shuffling over. He kept opening his mouth, and making sounds, but not words, really. No teeth — like something you'd read about in the *National Geographic*, maybe; the Appalachians, or the Dust Bowl . . . not somewhere this close to *Boston*."

"Did he give you anything?"

"Liza, come on. It was obvious. I just stuck a red heart through the crack of the door."

"Did you go to the house at the corner? That always looks so neat, as if nice people lived there."

"Yes, she was OK, older, kind of thin, but she had two little girls, very clean . . . baby-sitters, maybe, in a couple of years. She gave a dollar. Said she'd seen you out pushing Abby, wants you to stop by . . . if you're 'looking for company,' she said."

"Hunh. I might do that . . ." Liza thought it over.

"I think it would be a good idea," Julius said.

It turned out that Julius had not collected very much for the Heart Fund. He didn't say how much, and Liza didn't want to pin him down. He stopped talking, as if that were all he would say, but then he told her about the last place he'd been to.

"As soon as I pushed open the gate, all these dogs started rushing out at me — from inside the house, and from around back, everywhere. Half-breeds, all yapping, barking . . . skinny muzzles pointing right at me. I had to hold up my briefcase — to keep it out of their way. They all had these long tails curling up over their backs . . ."

"Oh, I've seen those dogs . . ." The dogs always made Abby laugh when Liza walked by there with her.

"Well, you wouldn't have liked it. And then the woman came out, and all these red-headed kids. I told her I was from the Heart Fund, and I held up a red heart so she wouldn't think I was a robber or something. Then she actually grabbed hold of my jacket. Her hair wasn't even combed. She kept calling me 'sir': 'Please, sir, help me, sir,' fixing me with her eyes. Then she said, 'He's no good,' pointing to her house. 'He just lays there; drunk, half the time he's drunk.' Then she said it was better when he *was* lying down. But the smell! I had to tear myself away from her."

"How *did* you?"

"I just said, 'I guess I came at a bad time.' Then I threw out all the red hearts I had left, and walked out the gate. Dogs were snapping at the hearts, kids grabbing for them. Over my shoulder I could see the woman following me, creeping along the chain link like a crab. I could hear her slippers flapping on the dirt. 'Sir, sir, please.' I had to go quite a way before I was finally out of earshot. And the dogs followed a way, too. I've never seen so many curling tails . . ."

Liza got up to clear the table. She didn't know why Julius minded so much about the tails. Those people are mostly just plain *poor*, Liza thought. Some fund or other should be collecting money for *them*. She didn't say that, of course, not wanting to upset Julius.

The next morning Julius told Liza that he was going to tell the Heart Fund people they should send letters next year. "With an envelope enclosed. Much more efficient."

A Letter

ABOUT ELEVEN each morning, before Abby's lunch, she and Liza would go out to the mailbox by the road to see what the mailman had brought. Before Abby learned to walk Liza would pull her in the little red wagon.

"Oh Abby, look, a letter from Grandpa."

Her father wrote her every Sunday, so it was not exactly a surprise when Liza spotted his clear blue script on a long white envelope. She read it while they made their way slowly back to the house.

Dear Liza,
I was glad to hear that you and Julius are well, and that Abby has recovered from her ear ache. Poor baby. And such a bright child! I wouldn't be surprised if she grew up to be a lawyer like her father. A girl can do almost anything these days, it seems, if she puts her mind to it. We have a delightful young lady (a Bryn Mawr graduate) at the bank now, in the trust department, and she seems to be doing a fine job.

Now, you mustn't worry about me. Of course, this house is empty without your mother. I can't seem to stop missing her.

Liza pictured her father alone in the house where he and her mother had always lived, where Liza had grown up. Had he learned to make coffee for one? He probably still had his dinner at the dining room table, the same as always. Afterward, would he play the piano, *Für Elise* and the first movement of the *Moonlight Sonata*, with no one to hear? A tear spotted the blue ink.

The letter went on,

> Bessie comes in every Tuesday as always, and keeps everything clean and neat. She always fixes something for my dinner. This week it was a chicken pot pie that lasted me for three nights. And a coconut cake, one of my favorites. At Prince's they have quite a variety of frozen foods that just need heating. The frozen fish sticks are very good, and one night I warmed up a TV dinner that was almost like Thanksgiving. It even had cranberry sauce! So you see I eat well.

Liza and Abby had reached the house, and Liza sank sobbing into a chair. Abby's eyes grew big.

"Oh, Abby, sometimes Mommies cry, too. Our poor darling Grandpa." She pulled Abby onto her lap and read the rest of the letter.

> I've gotten into the habit of walking downtown to the Blue Lantern for my dinner on Friday nights. Last Friday the hostess had just seated me when who should come in but Frank Bailey — Mr. Bailey, I suppose he is to you. He's alone now, too, so I invited him to join me. His daughter Doris (who was a few years ahead of you, I believe) lives now in Wheeling, West Virginia. She has *four* children, all boys, and quite a handful, I gather.

> This morning I spent an hour picking up twigs around the yard. We had quite a windstorm last night, but fortunately no big branches came down. Well, I must wind this up now, because your Aunt Lolly and Uncle Ferd have invited me over for dinner. So I'm well looked after.
>
> With love, and a special hug for Abby,
> Daddy

Liza had stopped crying, but with pain she pictured her father as she'd last seen him, his white shirt collar so loose now around his stringy neck.

"We'll get Grandpa to come for Christmas. How about that, my sweetie?" She picked Abby up and whirled her around in a little dance.

That night she gave Julius her father's letter to read. He and her father respected each other. Julius still called him Mr. Jackson.

"Well, that sounds all right," he said when Liza told him her plan for Christmas. "Can't see any reason why not."

Mr. & Mrs.

JULIUS AND Liza joined the Mr. & Mrs. Club in Rock Hill. Julius thought they should, and Liza looked forward to it. Anyone could go — any married couple, at least. Meetings were once a month, in the basement of the old church on the Common, up in the Center.

Peg Reilly, the woman who called Liza to invite them, said, "It's pot luck. Just bring a hot dish. Or a salad. Or a pie."

Liza decided to take Tuna Casserole, with potato chips on top. There was a lot of food, she thought, but by the end it was mostly gone. She and Julius sat at a table with the high school principal and his wife, Mr. and Mrs. Chorney. It turned out they'd both been to college, but not to any place Liza had heard of. Liza couldn't take her eyes off Ralph Chorney's sweater. A parade of antlered red and green moose wound drunkenly round and round his torso, up hill and down, through knitted fields of nubbly brown. He didn't look like a man who was used to wearing a sweater; his white shirt and dark tie peeked out at his throat.

"I made it," Estelle Chorney said proudly, patting her husband's lumpy sleeve.

"I thought so." Liza nodded.

The Mr. & Mrs. members seemed old to Liza, over thirty anyhow. Next to the Chorneys were Erford Pickens and his wife Mildred. Mildred had a little dead fur animal around her neck — a fox, Liza thought. The sharp teeth clamped on to the tail to hold it in place. Liza remembered her grandmother wearing a fox fur like that. Mildred wore it all during dinner. She was a substitute teacher; Erford was a farmer. In his spare time he was Dead Animal Inspector for the town. He'd been elected, and it meant that if you called him up, and said there was a smashed woodchuck on the road in front of your house, Erford Pickens would come in his truck and scrape it up. That seemed like a good thing to Liza, something she'd never really thought about before. After the Kitchen Committee finished the dishes, everyone played a game. If you didn't do something organized, Peg Reilly told Liza, all the men would get together and talk shop; the wives would talk about how many quarts of tomatoes they'd canned, stuff like that.

There were two teams. One person would be blindfolded, and someone from the other team would hold out some common household object, Peg told them. The blindfolded person had two minutes to guess what it was, just by asking yes or no questions.

Peg Reilly tied the blindfold on Julius; he had to take off his glasses. A big woman named Gladys something told him he could start guessing.

"Is it something you'd use in the kitchen?" he asked.

Gladys said yes.

"Would you use it every day?"

"Oh yes, every day."

Julius didn't know what it was even when he took his blindfold off. A potato masher. He'd never seen such a thing; Liza had never made mashed potatoes. She was embarrassed, and could feel her face turning pink, when everyone looked at her.

Julius didn't like the game much. "But it's a good way to meet people," he said to Liza on their way home. "Next month they're having a speaker."

"On what?" Liza wondered. Julius didn't know.

Games

JULIUS AND Liza were going to the Reillys' to play bridge.
They were asked for eight o'clock. This was the first time
they'd been invited to anyone's house in Rock Hill.
Socially, that is. "Don't get dressed up — nothing fancy,"
Peg Reilly had said on the phone. Julius decided to wear
just a casual shirt, no coat and tie. The only trouble was, he
didn't actually have any casual shirts — for the fall, at least
— so he put on one of his regular blue oxford button-
downs, leaving the top button undone. He kept looking in
the mirror, wondering, until Liza told him he looked just
perfect. She wore a plaid pleated skirt, with a white blouse
and red sweater.

Liza knew the basic rules of bridge, but she had never
liked it, and she wasn't very good at it. She just couldn't
seem to care about winning — which was, after all, the
whole point. Something was missing in her personality, she
decided: that competitive urge. It was the same with tennis;
for her, tennis had always been mainly social. Julius only
played bridge when they were visiting his mother, but he
played awfully well, in Liza's opinion. He had that knack of
being good at a lot of things he hardly ever did.

Everyone at the Reillys' was from the Mr. & Mrs. Club.
Ralph and Estelle Chorney, Gladys Shoemaker and her
husband Skip. Chipper Reilly was wearing plaid pants. Liza
had never seen a man in plaid pants before. He had a built-
in bar he'd made himself, out of an old sink. Liza knew she
should say something: "It's so shiny."

"Gee, thanks," Chipper said. "Just a lot of good old
elbow grease!" He turned to Julius. "What'll it be, old man?
Name your poison."

Everyone was drinking highballs. They all looked at
Liza when she said, "Just a coke for me, thanks." She didn't
want to make a fool of herself.

Two card tables with blue felt covers took up most of the Reillys' living room. Each table had a score pad with a cute little blue pencil hitched onto it, and new packs of cards decorated with flamingoes and palm trees.

Liza and Julius were at the table with the Reillys, but Julius was Peg's partner, and Liza teamed with Chipper. The first few hands went all right; Liza's cards were pretty dull, and she kept a low profile. Then she got a hand with a lot of face cards, and she knew she had to say something. "No trump." She wasn't sure what to do, and it went all wrong. Chipper pretended he didn't mind, but his face got all red, and he started guzzling Party-Mix, so Liza knew he did. Peg was really good, so she and Julius cleaned up. Liza hoped they wouldn't have to do this very often, but we probably will, she thought.

They played for a long time. Liza sneaked a peek at her watch when she was dummy, then missed some clues from Chipper when he had a fantastic hand, so he went down three.

"I had almost every heart in the deck," he said afterward. "An incredible hand! Once in a lifetime . . . but don't feel bad, Liza."

Liza felt terrible. Julius was annoyed at her, too, she could tell, even though he'd won.

She expected they could go home when they finally stopped playing bridge. It was after midnight. But the four women went out to the kitchen, where Peg uncovered a three-layer fudge cake and a strawberry cheesecake. They all helped carry things onto the lace-covered table in the dining room, where Peg poured coffee into flowered cups.

"You haven't lost your touch, girl," Chipper called to Peg with his mouth full of cake. Liza saw Peg smile while everyone complimented her on the cakes. The men all sat at one end of the table. Liza could hear Ralph Chorney going on about cylinders and horsepower, things Julius was not much up on, she knew.

Gladys had canned more tomatoes than anyone else. "Forty-two quarts," she told them. To Liza it sounded like "foughty-two quats." She still wasn't used to the way people in Rock Hill left out the R's. Gladys had made so much strawberry jam that she was thinking of setting up a little stand at the end of their driveway. Peg had frozen fifty-eight quarts of beans and almost as much corn. Liza said she'd been freezing stuff, too, but didn't mention that she had done only four packages of beans, which seemed like a lot at the time.

"Rock Hill is a lot different from Cambridge," Julius said later. "Maybe you should take bridge lessons, Liza. Otherwise we'll never fit in."

Bridge lessons! Aha, she thought: a chance, maybe, to go in to Cambridge once in a while.

LIZA'S FATHER wouldn't come for Christmas, even though she and Julius had both invited him. "You should have just your own little family for your first Christmas in your new (old) house," he wrote. "Please don't worry about me. I could come up for the New Year's weekend, if it suits you, especially since it's little Abby's first birthday. But tell me honestly if you have other plans."

Her father would take the day train, leaving Philadelphia at 8 a.m., he wrote, arriving in Boston at 4:47. Then he'd walk, he said, to Julius's office, and they could ride out to Rock Hill together.

"I'd like to meet him," Liza told Julius. "I could drive down with Abby to that new station they have on Route 128."

She telephoned her father to explain the change of plan. He couldn't quite understand why a railroad station would be named after a highway.

"Well, it's not much of a station, actually, but all of the trains stop there now because of the new highway. It'll be a little bit shorter ride for you, and we can talk all the way home, and then have tea."

Everything was settled until that Friday morning, the day her father was to travel. The sky was iron gray, with lowering clouds, and no wind. Julius flicked on the radio in the kitchen while they had their oatmeal. "Snow is expected," they heard. "Significant accumulation . . . a travellers' advisory . . ."

"When is it supposed to start?" asked Liza. But no one said.

"I think we should tell him to go on into Boston, after all." Julius looked even more solemn that usual. "I don't want you and Abby getting caught in the storm."

"But it's too late!" wailed Liza. "He would have left already."

"Well then, *I'll* meet him," Julius said, and that was that.

By lunchtime it was snowing hard. Liza put Abby down for her nap, but found herself unable to concentrate on anything. The radio crackled with news of the storm, and nothing else. Liza called Julius at his office. "Don't *worry*, Liza. I'll be fine. I have snow tires and a full tank of gas, and I'll leave in plenty of time. Just *relax*, will you? And fix us a good dinner, not one of your casseroles, OK?"

Meatloaf is what we're having, she said to herself after she hung up. And you'd better like it.

She was not relaxed at all. She made another phone call, or tried to. The number of the new station, when she finally got it from the operator, was busy, busy. There was nothing to do but look out the window. After the early darkness fell she stared at the white flakes flying thick and fast through the path of light shining from the porch. Once in a while a snow plow would rumble past. She thought of trying to shovel a path, but she couldn't leave Abby. She called every railroad number she could find; all busy.

It was after six when the phone rang. She heard Julius, crackly, static-y. "I'm at a Howard Johnson's. I couldn't get through. The whole highway is stalled, you wouldn't believe how bad it is, but I finally got to an exit. Now I'm heading home. I'll get there when I get there. Don't wait up."

"But *Julius*! What about Daddy?"

"There's nothing I can do, Liza. You don't understand, it's really bad. Look, I've got to hang up; there's a line for the phone."

Sick with worry, Liza pictured her fragile father shivering in a stalled train somewhere in the wilds of

Connecticut. She gave Abby her bath and sang the usual good-night songs, all the while framing the furious sentences she knew she'd never say to Julius.

Three hours later, Julius, looking like a snowman, came stamping into the house. He was cold, weary, and cross. He poured himself some Four Roses, and sat down to the meat-loaf, potatoes, and peas that Liza dished up for him. He didn't seem to feel like talking.

"You must be exhausted, Julius." He's probably worried about Daddy, too, even though he won't show it, she thought. "Would you like another slice of meatloaf?" She tried to sound calm, but her voice came out wavery and shrill.

"Relax, Liza, how do we know your father's not holed up snug and warm at the Copley Plaza by now? Don't worry! We'll hear soon."

"Julius, you know he isn't! He would have called. And trains can get stuck, too."

"Trains can go through anything." He pushed his plate away. "I don't want to talk about it. And after all I've been through, there's nothing more I can do."

Liza couldn't sleep at all. She left the porch light on, as though her father might magically appear on their doorstep. She tried to read the new Graham Greene, but it was no use. The radio told of pile-ups, abandoned cars, and power outages. At seven a.m., when the phone rang, it was still snowing.

"Liza?" Her father sounded hoarse. And weak.

"Daddy! Where *are* you?"

"Oh, I'm still here, at Route 128. Have you heard from Julius? I've been so worried about him."

"Daddy, he's home. He said he couldn't get to you. I feel terrible. I hope you could stretch out on a bench, at least."

"No, no benches. It's very crowded. I've just been standing."

"All night?" Liza was frantic. "Oh, Daddy, have you had anything to eat?" Julius was talking at her, too, from his side of the bed. Liza covered one ear and tried to hear her father.

"Oh yes, a nice Italian lady had a cake she was taking to her son, and she shared it with all of us. But what shall I do now, Liza? I didn't want to wake you up. They say a train may come through soon, heading into Boston. Do you think I should get on it?"

"A train to Boston?"

"Liza," Julius was saying. "Tell him to get on that train."

"I can hardly hear you, Daddy."

"Here, let me talk to him." Julius pulled the phone away.

"Hello Mr. Jackson. This is quite an adventure for you, isn't it? Storm of the century, they're saying. Now, here's what to do . . ."

"Adventure," sputtered Liza.

Julius told Liza's father to try to get to Boston, and then find a cab, if he could, to take him to the other station, where he could catch a train to the stop near Rock Hill.

"Call me when you get there, sir, and I'll try to meet you."

"Daddy . . ." Liza grabbed the phone back.

"Everybody wants to use the phone, Liza. I have to say good-bye."

While Julius cleared a track from the door, and shovelled out his car, Liza fixed the oatmeal and fed Abby. When Julius came in they didn't speak. Liza talked to Abby, sipped her coffee, and tried to read the paper.

"I'd like a boiled egg, too, Liza," Julius said. Liza cooked the egg for him, exactly four minutes, and set it before him without a word.

It was close to ten when the phone rang. Julius picked it up. "Good. Look for me in about twenty minutes, Mr. Jackson."

When Liza finally saw her father trudging slowly up the path, she ran out. Oh, he looks so thin, she thought, so frail.

Even his face is gray. A breeze might tip him over. When she put her arms around him he felt like a bundle of twigs inside his gray coat.

He patted Abby on the head. Liza offered him coffee and a nip of brandy, which he took. He said he wasn't hungry. Liza had a hard time persuading him to put on his pajamas and get into bed.

"Oh, no, no," he said at first. "Not yet, it's still morning." But he gave in. "Well, maybe you're right. I'll have my bath later." It was already dark when he woke up.

Liza didn't speak to Julius all day. Finally he said, "You know Liza, I really couldn't help it. The highway was totally blocked."

"I believe you, Julius, but at least you could have acted as if you *cared*. He's my *father*, and he's 74 years old."

"I'm sorry, Liza."

His face was down, but his eyes looked up at her, his hands twisted together. He looked, Liza decided, as though he really were sorry. She wasn't sure she'd ever heard Julius apologize before. For anything. She melted just a trifle, and held out her hand. Julius put his arms around her shoulders, and patted her on the back. A good moment.

By the next day her father was his old cheerful self. He even made light of his long night in the crowded railway station.

"No one could leave, even if they had a car parked outside. One fellow kept saying, 'I could sure use a drink. Doesn't anyone have a bottle we could share?' No one did, but then — I had to laugh — about three hours later, who should open up his briefcase and pull out a full bottle of Old Grandad? Of course he had to pass it around; served him right, ha-ha!"

They celebrated Abby's birthday, the four of them, and wished each other Happy New Year. Liza had made a devil's food cake from a mix, knowing it was a favorite of her father's. One candle. Liza's father had brought a doll for Abby, the kind that had pink cheeks, yellow yarn hair, and a blue dress if you held it one way, and a brown face, black hair, and a red checked dress when you flipped it over.

"She'll need two names," Liza said.

"How about 'Snowy' and 'Stormy'"? Liza's father smiled at his own little joke, but Abby used those names from then on.

At the Country Club

IN MAY Liza and Julius went to the last Mr. & Mrs. meeting of the season. It wasn't a meeting, really; everyone met at the Mammoth Country Club in the town next to Rock Hill. Peg and Chipper Reilly belonged to the country club, so that was how the Mr. & Mrs. Club could have its annual outing there.

Everyone was quite dressed up. Chipper Reilly was wearing his plaid pants and white shoes. Mildred Pickens had on red high heels with open toes, a flowered dress with pearls, and her fur piece.

They had cocktails out on the terrace; Liza ordered a Tom Collins. A waitress passed little hot meatballs on toothpicks. Julius started talking to a man he recognized from law school. Tom Ryan had been two years ahead of Julius. Julius couldn't believe it, and neither could Liza, but it was true. Tom and his wife Billie Ray had just bought an old house in Rock Hill. Now there would be two men commuting to Boston.

Billie talked with Liza. She had a southern accent, and was shorter than Liza, who had to bend over to hear what she was saying. Liza wasn't sure if Billie was pregnant, or just overweight. She had a sleeveless black coat on over her dress, and a little black cap pinned on her head. Her hair was twisted into two little buns, one behind each ear. She looks old-fashioned, Liza thought — sort of like Ma in the Laura Ingalls Wilder books. She was not like any of the law school wives Liza had known in Cambridge. Probably it's because she's older — and southern, Liza decided.

Julius was still talking to Tom, and they were laughing. Billie was asking Liza what she did all day, about her baby, whether she missed Cambridge. Billie's big brown eyes beseeched; she seemed so needy, so pleading — desperate, almost, although Liza knew that was ridiculous. She took a step back, not wanting to be rude, but they were supposed to mix. She turned toward two women who were talking about their tennis lessons.

Everyone lined up for the buffet. A man in a huge white hat sliced the roast beef. You could have it rare or well done, as thick as you wanted. Dessert was mint parfait with a maraschino cherry on top. Liza didn't think it was as good as it looked; mostly vanilla ice cream, really.

Later, Liza and Julius happened to leave at the same time as Spider and Tilly Follen. Spider was even taller than Julius, and Tilly was tiny. Tilly was so . . . shapely, with more makeup than the other wives. Liza couldn't help noticing her sparkly gold ankle bracelet. But Peg Reilly had told Liza that Tilly's mother was the third grade teacher at Abner E. Dornbush Elementary, so Tilly *couldn't* be a tart, really, even though that's what she looked like.

Spider came around the circle in a two-tone blue convertible with the top down. Julius held the door open, and Tilly hopped in.

"He works at a Buick dealership," Julius told Liza as they drove home in the Henry J. "Wouldn't you know he was a car salesman?" Liza didn't know any car salesmen. She was thinking maybe she should try some mascara; she'd noticed Maybelline on a rack at the Atomic Super Market.

"It was great running into Tom." Julius sounded happy. "The last person I expected to see in Rock Hill. He works at Loring and Gould; corporate stuff, mostly. We should have them over for dinner soon, okay?"

When they reached home, Julius waited in the car while Liza went in and paid Peggy Sue the babysitter. Four hours. Then Liza had a few minutes by herself before Julius got back. She didn't really do anything, just stood by the sink, wiping off the clean counter.

Bread Rising

EVER SINCE the gala Mr. & Mrs. Club dinner at the Mammoth Country Club, Liza kept envisioning Billie Ray Ryan in her little black cap, with those big brown eyes looking up, entreating, seeking something. Liza felt herself pulling back just remembering, but somehow couldn't get Billie out of her head.

One day two weeks later, when the phone rang, Liza guessed it would be Billie Ray.

"Do you remember me? Our husbands know each other, and I thought we should become acquainted. I'd be happy if you'd come over for a visit with your little girl. She might like to play with my boys."

Billie had no car, but Liza did, so they agreed that Liza and Abby would come over the next afternoon at four.

When she opened her door, Billie bent over Abby. "Hello darlin'; you're a mighty sweet little girl. Now boys, you be nice to Abby; treat her like a lady. Duane, you look after them, hear me?"

The two boys, Thurman and Donny, were older than Abby, probably three and four. Their big sister Duane, a slender, pale, serious little girl, might have been eight. She led Abby off with the boys.

Billie's brown hair was smooth, neatly braided and coiled behind her ears. Pans of bread and rolls were rising under dish towels in the kitchen. Open shelves were crowded with old crocks, black iron skillets, thick white plates.

"Would you care for some ice tea?" Billie asked. "Unless you prefer Pepsicola. I have a fondness for Pepsicola."

Liza and Billie took their drinks into the sparsely-furnished living room. Everything was old. "Just country pieces," Billie told Liza. "I go to farm auctions, then I strip everything out in the yard."

Liza's eyes followed Billie's arm as she gestured out the window. Sure enough, there was a battered blue table, waiting for Billie to attack it. Liza looked around the room at the pallid bleached chairs and chests. The sofa and chairs were covered with pillows and quilts. Liza sat down in a rocking chair.

"What time does your husband get home at night?" asked Billie. "Tom never comes in till around eight, and I don't see him in the morning; he's gone before I wake up. I'm the kind that needs her sleep."

"Does he go in on Saturdays, too? Julius sometimes has to work Saturdays."

"Un-hunh, Saturdays, too. So how long have you been here in Rock Hill? Do you like it here? Made any friends? I'd like for you and me to be friends; it seems like kind of a lonely place, not neighborly like home . . ." Billie was from West Virginia. She sighed, and popped open another bottle of Pepsi.

Liza heard a mournful whistle, and then the loud clatter of a freight train that came rattling right behind the Ryans' house, past the blue table, the tire swing, the bleak little garage.

"I'm always thinking I'd just love to hop right on that old freight train, go wherever it took me," Billie mused. Then she laughed, and flapped her hand in front of her face as if she were brushing away a fly.

"I don't mind the noise of the freight trains, though, not like those old Army planes that buzz over here all the time. Last week I called up the base — I used to be an Army bride. 'I want to talk to the Commanding Officer,' I told the sergeant. 'Well, ma'am,' he said, 'I'll let you speak to the Officer of the Day.' I told that sergeant, 'I don't want to talk to any gold-bricking O.D.; I want your Commanding Officer.'"

"So then what?" Liza leaned forward.

"Oh I got him all right. I said, 'Colonel, your boys are waking up my babies with their blankety-blank C-47s flying right over my house. You've gotta send them somewhere else.' He said, 'Ma'am, don't you worry, I'll see to it,' and he did. You have to be tough in this world." She struggled to her feet.

They went to the kitchen. Billie's bread was in the oven. Liza inhaled the sweet warm smell.

"I wish I could make bread. It seems so . . . domestic," Liza said. "I'm not very good at all those things."

"Well, I have to. It's the only way I can get bread for Tom's lunches and Duane's. Anyway, Tom won't eat store bread. But you know, the truth is I don't mind. A lot of times, kneading it, I start crying . . . but then I figure with the tears I hardly need to use any salt."

When it was time to go, Billie wrapped a warm loaf in a clean dish towel. "Please, Liza. I want you all to have this. It did me good having you come over."

Duane led Abby down the stairs. "Bye Abby," the boys called. "Come back tomorrow! Can she, Mama?"

"Thank you for looking after Abby," Liza said. Duane stood there, straight and unsmiling, like a little soldier. Billie stood in the door while the boys waved from the steps.

45

At the Prom

"BAH THE deep . . . da da ta-da,
And pearly waters . . . ta-da dot da . . ."
The gym was festooned with blue and white crepe paper streamers. Liza and Julius were chaperones at the high school prom. Everyone on the School Committee was supposed to be there with their wives, but Puggy and Pearl Swenson were the only others who had shown up. Of course Mr. and Mrs. Chorney were there — he was the principal — and some of the teachers.

The band consisted of Tinker Whiting (who ran the garage) on drums, and three other guys, all from Rock Hill. One of them was singing a song that Liza liked in a deep bass voice: ". . .white silver sands." He even had the accent right, kind of southern drawlish.

Mrs. Chorney had told Liza that she should check the Girls' Room every half hour or so, just to keep an eye. A couple of chubby girls seemed to be camped out there for good, while others kept whipping in and out breathlessly, checking their ponytails, applying another coat of silvery-pink to bee-stung lips, and hitching up their flouncy strapless dresses. Liza looked in the mirror. She felt dowdy in the narrow green dress that had seemed so glamorous when it was new. Was that only three years ago? Her permanented hair, too, seemed old and flat-looking. Mrs. Chorney had brought a pink hand mirror and a brush and comb set from home. Liza lined them up again on the counter and threw away some crumpled, lipsticky tissues. Then she went back to the music.

". . . you got me singin' the blues." The chaperones all stood in a group in one corner. None of them was dancing.

"Not exactly our kind of music, is it? Heh, heh." That was Mr. Chorney, who must have been at least forty. No one disagreed with him.

"Lord, no," said Pearl Swenson. Her breasts bounced when she laughed.

It *is* my kind of music, Liza thought, though she'd never admit it, especially to Julius. He was very fussy about music, and he didn't like to dance anyway.

When the band played a slow number Mr. Chorney walked across the floor, tapping the shoulders of couples who were dancing too close. The wives and Miss Crawford the Home Ec teacher brought out bowls of pink punch and trays of chocolate chip cookies. Liza helped line up miniature paper cups; she fanned out the blue paper napkins.

During the band's break, a student group took the stage for a couple of numbers, turning up the amps. "Oh he's a long, tall Texan . . ." Some of the kids started dancing that new way, not touching, waggling their hips, elbows flying, shaking their fists. ". . . in a tin gallon hay-at." Liza longed to be out there. Her foot was tapping before she realized someone might notice.

Mrs. Chorney had her hands over her ears and a rueful smile on her face. Mr. Chorney was about to tap the musicians on their shoulders, but luckily the real band came strolling back just in the nick of time. The chaperones settled down again, sighing with relief. "Oh youngsters these days . . . whoo-ee." Mr. Chorney sent Julius to check around, make sure no couples had sneaked outside.

It just happened that Julius was gone when Larry LaComb walked over and asked Liza if she'd care to dance. Black-haired Larry worked at Tinker's gas station; his father was the one who pumped out Julius and Liza's septic tank.

Mrs. Chorney smiled, so Liza thought it was all right if she danced with Larry LaComb. He was on the football team, and vice-president of his class, definitely not a hood or anything like that.

"Ah'm gonna sit right down and write mahself a letter . . ."

Liza's eyes were riveted on Larry LaComb's ruffled

shirt front. He was wearing a powder blue cummerbund with a tie to match. He smelled of Old Spice and sweat, like a football player; dancing was hard work. She looked up at his black sideburns and the hair that had started to curl from dampness. He was humming into Liza's ear.

". . . and make believe it came from you."

When the song ended, he bowed to Liza. "Thank you very much, Mrs. Prescott."

Oh. Well, naturally he would call her Mrs. Prescott. What else? But still . . . She felt a little subdued as he walked her back to the chaperones' corner. She couldn't help seeing two blonde girls, their bare shoulders touching, their tanned faces turned toward Liza. Each had a hand up to her mouth. They were laughing. At her.

Mrs. Chorney looked at her shoes as Liza rejoined the group. "Well, well," said Julius. No one else said anything.

Finally the band was playing "Good-night Sweetheart," and the chaperones lined up at the door to shake everyone's hand.

On the way home in the car Julius was silent. Just as Liza was about to go in to get Peggy Sue the babysitter, he said, "Liza, please don't do that again, dancing with the students. None of the other chaperones . . ."

"Oh . . . , don't *worry!*" Liza ran toward the house, letting the car door slam.

Flags

BUNNY HOPKINS was coming for Memorial Day weekend. Julius and Bunny had been roommates at college. Bunny lived in New York and had something to do with the Metropolitan Museum.

"Bunny can't stand children," Julius said.

"So. Then why is he coming?" asked Liza.

"Don't be like that, Liza. I just wanted to remind you, so you'd sort of keep Abby under wraps. You know."

"Yeah, I do know. It sounds like a great weekend." Even so, she looked forward to seeing Bunny; he always made her laugh.

Bunny loved their house.

"Oh this is charming; it's so . . . *American*! Liza, you have a real touch; I adore it."

Liza was not sure "American" was a compliment, coming from Bunny.

Later, after they'd said goodnight, Bunny appeared in the kitchen in his silky black dressing gown. Liza noticed that he was still wearing his paisley ascot.

"*Would* you mind — another blanket? I'm absolutely *ruined* by my apartment in the city, steam heat and all. Not used to this marvelous country air." He inhaled deeply of the air in the Prescotts' kitchen. "I hate to be a bore . . ."

Liza went upstairs to find a blanket.

"Thanks, darling, ever so. Nigh' night!"

After breakfast they drove up to the center of Rock Hill to watch the Memorial Day parade. Julius carried Abby on his shoulders.

"This town! I'm crazy about it, what a gem," Bunny said. "So New England. And all the flags. Fabulous."

Bunny joined right in with the crowd. He seemed carried away by the ranks of uniformed Boy Scouts, then the Girl Scouts, with their leaders wearing larger versions of the same uniforms, all marching more or less smartly to the drum beats of the high school band. White-booted baton twirlers preceded the red-clad band members, who, just as they passed by Bunny and the Prescotts, launched into a wailing rendition of "The Stars and Stripes Forever," slightly off key. Liza saw Bunny close his eyes, and tilt his head back, as though transported. As she turned the other way Liza noticed a man who looked different from most of the men in Rock Hill. His clean khakis, white button-down shirt, and lean serious face set him apart. He stood alone by an elm tree. Somehow Liza's glance met his, and she looked away, conscious of her face turning pink.

A man in a three-cornered hat rode by on a horse, followed by five or six grizzled men in old fashioned soldiers' uniforms, walking, smiling and waving to the crowd. Last of all in the parade came a car that Liza recognized — an enormous open convertible, blue and white, driven at a stately pace by Spider the Buick dealer. A sign on the side of the car said "Gold Star Mothers." The four silver-haired women in the car were laughing, joking with Spider, calling out to their friends — having, it seemed, the time of their lives.

Bunny flung an arm around Liza. "I don't believe this!" he said. "Don't you *adore* it?"

Drawing away, Liza said, "Actually, I think it's sort of sad." Julius just looked bored.

By the Civil War cannon, the Colonial Minute Men began firing off their muskets. Abby and all the other little children screamed. Liza pulled Abby from Julius and walked with her away from the noise. She ran into Peg Reilly, there with her brood. "Did you see Tina? She marched with the Brownies. We're so proud of Big Sister, aren't we kids?"

"Peg, who's that guy back there, by the elm? Do you know him?"

"That's Derek Clifford — you know who they are — the granite people. I don't actually know them, but he's the youngest, the black sheep supposedly. Why did you want to know?"

"I just wondered." Liza wished she hadn't asked.

"Okay kiddos, no more bangs, no more parade," Peg said. "Let's go find Tina. Bye, Abby — see you, Liza."

From a vendor Liza bought a small flag for Abby to hold, then rejoined Julius and Bunny, walking to the car.

By the time they got home, clouds had parted and the sun was warm. Liza gave Abby her lunch, put her down for a nap, and then carried their late lunch out into the garden, where the last of her nearly black tulips were still blooming. She'd been working to have the garden look its best, knowing Bunny would notice.

Julius had opened a bottle of wine. He and Bunny, in the Adirondack chairs, were drinking and talking when Liza came out with the tray of sandwiches. Julius looked cross and Bunny was frowning. Liza caught the end of what Bunny was saying.

"Yeah, I know, I know, but he's more than a friend, actually . . ." Bunny quickly composed his features when he saw her.

What have they been talking about, Liza wondered.

"Oh Liza, Liza, you're a dream. Liebfraumilch and — don't tell me — chicken sandwiches. Heaven! And what is that, a little Brie? Jules, you lucky dog, does she always treat you this well?"

Julius grunted in reply. Liza handed out plates and paper napkins.

51

"Your little garden's so sweet, Lize; I can tell you've been trying."

Julius sat up. "What do you mean 'trying'? Look at her fingernails. I didn't even get any *lunch* on Saturday till two o'clock. Liza was out here slaving away."

Liza didn't say anything. She looked at her nails, still grimy.

Bunny helped himself to more cheese. "So Liza, we *both* think you're terrific," he said. "That parade was divine, wasn't it? The whole scene . . . You know I just realized. I used to know a guy who was actually *from* Rock Hill — Hammy Clifford; we were pretty good friends then, but sort of drifted apart after college. Do you remember him, Jules? Big bucks there — the family granite business. I went to his sister's coming-out party — quite a blast, no holds barred."

"I've heard of the Cliffords," Liza said. "And I know where they live."

"Le Pigeonnier, a real pile; fabulous garden, too. I should give them a bell while I'm here — see if Hammy's in town."

But after lunch he went to sleep.

Julius had cheered up by dinner time. He and Bunny laughed and gossiped about people they'd known at college. Whatever happened to old so-and-so? Julius would ask. Bunny always seemed to know, and it was always something outrageous, like going off to join a Trappist monastery, or conning poor Bedouins out of their best rugs and then selling them to a high-priced decorator, or running discreet errands for ambassadors' beautiful wives in Paris or Buenos Aires. Liza put her head back and laughed. Bunny didn't mention the Cliffords again, and somehow Liza didn't either.

The next morning Bunny, clutching his tie, rushed into the kitchen while Julius and Abby were spooning up their oatmeal. With his hair still damp from the shower, he sprinkled wet droplets over Liza when he hugged her.

"No, no thanks, dearie, just coffee for me. Black." Bunny tied his red-dotted necktie, but he wouldn't sit down. "Do you always leave this early, Jules?"

Then Julius was dashing out to the car, heading for his office, and taking Bunny to a train back to New York.

"Be sure to let me know when you're in the City," Bunny said, as he pecked Liza's cheek. "I'll show you things at the Met that you've *never* seen," he murmured. "And a little night life, some jazz. You must be starved for the bright lights — both of you."

Liza and Abby waved from the doorstep. When Liza went to pull the sheets off Bunny's bed, she found he'd left his little red leather address book under a pillow. She checked under "C" to see if Ham Clifford were listed in it. He was. Liza wondered if Bunny had forgotten about calling the Cliffords, or had he thought better of it? But now Bunny was gone, and the opportunity was gone, and she felt sad. Oh, well. She gathered up sheets and towels and stuffed them briskly into the washing machine.

"Let's go outside, punkin — it's warm! We don't even need our sweaters. Come on, Abby-kins, I'll push you on the swing."

Bounty from South of the Border

JULIUS'S MOTHER was coming for her first visit to Rock Hill. "Two nights, dearie," she'd told Liza on the phone. "That'll be long enough, you wait and see. *And* enough for me, too!" She laughed, that husky cigarette laugh that ended in a wheeze.

Julius called his mother "Ma," but to everyone else, including Liza, she was "Minx," short for Marian, a name no one used. Minx lived in New York. Julius met her plane after work and drove her out to Rock Hill.

From the window of Abby's room, Liza watched their arrival. Minx's floppy-brimmed straw hat and green harlequin sunglasses hid her face. She staggered up the flagstone path in her high heels — always high ones to make herself taller — tan toothpick legs, narrow red dress like one stroke of a crayon. Her usual huge leather satchel hung from one shoulder, making her list to one side like a stalk of hollyhock in a strong wind. Julius trudged behind in his heavy brown crepe-soled shoes, Minx's suitcase in one hand, his briefcase in the other.

"Abby, pet, come to Minx." She squatted down, dropping her bag, flinging out her arms. Abby cowered behind Liza. Silver bracelets clanked as Minx struggled to her feet, tottering, then reaching up to embrace Liza.

"You look terrible, dearie; white as a fish belly, and skinnier than ever. Don't you ever get out in the sun? You need a break, and so does Jules. Can't you get more help? So when he comes home after a long day at the office you can be more . . . Did I send Abby that dress? Too short already, I see."

They walked slowly toward the guest room.

"Ooh, what a ghastly drive. I can't think why you two wanted to move to the absolute end of the world."

Minx dropped her bag and her hat on the bed. Liza had put an ashtray on every surface in the room. She'd spent most of the morning ironing the ruffled organdy curtains, tearing a couple of corners when the starch got stuck. She'd never tried starch before.

"Oh, this is so sweet," laughed Minx. "And you do it all yourself! I always knew you were the kind of girl who'd make a bed with the sheets so tight, not a single wrinkle. Aren't I right?"

Was that supposed to be a compliment? Liza didn't feel the way you usually do when someone praises you. She watched as the ash fell from Minx's cigarette.

Later Minx came into the kitchen wearing an orange caftan with purple birds embroidered on it.

"Isn't it divine? I found the most heavenly little shop in Acapulco . . ." Minx had recently come back from Mexico. She had her arms full of paper parcels.

"Here's your martini, Ma." Julius poured from the silver shaker, just polished by Liza. Abby was in her high chair, spoon poised over applesauce.

"We'll all watch Liza cook," Minx said, sinking onto the window seat. "Abby, pet, here's a surprise from your old Minx."

Abby looked bewildered until Minx pulled off the string, releasing a little purple smock with pink birds on it. The smock fell into the applesauce. Liza came over from the stove to unwrap her own larger matching smock. Julius's present was a yellow tie printed with orange flowers.

"Ma! When do you expect me to wear this?" Julius held the tie well out in front of him.

"You won't believe it, but when we were in Acapulco I

ran into a terribly attractive pair who turned out to live in this town — Rocky whatever."

Minx was starting in on her second martini, alternately smoking and eating the cheese wafers Liza had made from a little jar of Olde English cheese spread.

"It was too killing. We were all in this little shop, trying on these marvelous things, and talking. When I heard she was from Massachusetts, of course I said I had a son there — in a tiny little town in the middle of nowhere. She said, 'Well I live in a little town,' and then I just couldn't believe it when she said Rock Hill."

Liza was surprised that someone from Rock Hill had travelled to Acapulco. Julius sat up straight.

"What was this woman's name?"

"Her husband was there, too, waiting out in their car, and *not* looking happy. They're the Cliffords — he's the head of a big granite company, she said, an old family business. Does that ring a bell? Anyhow, they know I'm here now, and they want us for a drink tomorrow." She held out her empty glass toward Julius.

"Clifford Granite! Theirs is the big yellow house, with a tennis court and a lot of trees, up near the common." He shook his head, and gave a little laugh. "Bunny Hopkins was talking about them, too. Funny."

Julius's mother has hardly been here an hour, Liza thought, and already everything seems different. She looked at Minx, wondering how long before the next ash would drop.

Chicks

WHEN THEY turned into the Cliffords' sweeping gravel driveway the next afternoon, Liza felt butterflies inside. A small black sign said "Le Pigeonnier" in gold letters. "What the hell does *that* mean?" asked Julius.

Minx pulled a mirrored compact from her shiny red bag. "It's just the name of their place, dear," dabbing at her nose with orange powder. "It doesn't have to mean anything."

"Hunh. Why pigeons?"

Julius and his mother argued about which door they should use. At what was obviously the front of the big yellow house, the wide black door was flanked by pots, one at either side, each holding a tree shaped like a perfect lollipop. Liza wanted to go up close, tap the shiny brass lion's head knocker. But Minx, pencil slim in sleeveless black, strode on high sandals toward the other door, this one flanked by dog dishes and L.L. Bean boots. A rope dangled from a brass bell above the door.

"No, no, this is obviously the kitchen door," Julius whispered.

"Oh Jules, don't be an oaf. Obviously they want people to come in this way." Minx did not whisper. She took Abby's hand and walked to the house.

Julius stood by the car as though rooted, tall and stiff, tilted back slightly, Liza noticed, on his heavy brown shoes.

But then the door opened, and Mrs. Clifford, looped with ropes of colorful beads, was whooping a welcome to Minx. They hugged each other as if they were old friends. Mrs. Clifford was no taller than Minx, but dumpier in her flowery sack dress. Her bare brown-freckled arms, soft and flabby, flung around Minx's narrow shoulders, made Liza think of birthday balloons the morning after, when most of the air had leaked out. Amid noisy introductions, and a babbling stream of chatter, they all moved into what *was* the kitchen, and definitely the way they were expected to enter this world that seemed so apart from everything else in Rock Hill.

Coming in from the sunset glare it was so dark that Liza couldn't see at first the three other people in the room.

"This is my son Ham," Mrs. Clifford said, "and Evvy, and my little sweetie pie Hammy." She tickled the chin of the plump baby that Evvy was holding.

Liza caught a glimpse of another man who looked like Ham, younger, dressed like him in a blue blazer and striped tie. The man she had seen at the parade. But her attention went to Evvy, whom she knew.

"Evvy," she said. "I don't believe it! What a surprise to see you here."

"I live here," Evvy said, not sounding as surprised as Liza.

"Don't tell me! You girls know each other. How marvelous!" Mrs. Clifford chattered on.

Liza and Evvy had been together at college, friendly but not friends; then Liza dropped out to marry Julius. She'd used to think Evvy was silly, not a serious person. Now they compared their lives since college, their husbands, their babies.

"Ham and I got married at Thanksgiving, the usual big deal," Evvy told her. "Since then we've been living here with Ham's parents, until the company — Clifford Granite — gets around to fixing up a house for us. I can't wait."

Evvy's baby was three months old. Liza couldn't stop herself from counting months, and couldn't help being shocked. Evvy didn't seem to be embarrassed. Liza turned, finally, to the other man, standing there, silent, dragging on a cigarette, watching and listening to her and Evvy.

"Hi, I'm Derek." He held out his hand, smiling at her, a half smile. Derek was taller than his older brother; both he and Ham had the same sharp chiselled faces. Liza felt his warm hand on hers for half a second.

"We should go in the other room," Evvy said.

They all walked through the dining room, dense with dim portraits, dark mahogany, and a sideboard weighed down with silver. In the hall was a glass-fronted, lighted cabinet, filled with guns. They walked on, toward the sound of voices and laughter.

The big sitting room was flooded with afternoon light from long windows. Liza noticed a grand piano and two fireplaces. Like a country club, she thought. She walked across an expanse of oriental carpet toward the brown leather chair where Mr. Clifford sat with his feet on a hassock. He didn't rise when Mrs. Clifford introduced Liza.

Ham was making drinks for everyone at a mirrored bar in a corner of the room. On the wall next to the bar was a large oil painting of a nude woman, tones of orange and a triangle of black, sprawled against turquoise cushions and sniffing a pink rose.

"Holy cow," said Julius, staring.

"That's Ma," Ham said in a neutral tone, as he busied himself among the bottles.

Julius whirled around to look again at Mrs. Clifford. Liza looked at the rug.

"Marvelous," Minx said. "Rather Matisse, don't you think?"

"Simon Sutton, old friend of the family," said Mr. Clifford. "Best thing he ever did."

Liza had a hard time imagining dumpy little Mrs. Clifford in that particular pose. Ham and Derek both looked like their father, she decided, though Mr. Clifford had sagging jowls and clipped hair like a gray rug. With their straight noses and jutting chins they would fit right in on Mount Rushmore. E. Hampton Clifford, hewn from rock. The baby was probably E. Hampton the Third.

Mr. Clifford was talking to Minx. "I bet you've never even heard of the Restigouche. Best fishing river in Canada, that's all. We just have a plain old fishing camp, Indian guides, the works. Get up there every year for a week or so. Catch your limit every day, have a great time, plenty of booze and no *women*, that's the best part, ha ha."

"Now, now, Hampton — may I call you that? — think how much more fun you could have if . . ." Minx's bracelets clinked; her red nails flashed. She was flirting with Mr. Clifford. Liza turned away.

Mrs. Clifford was showing Abby an antique-looking doll in an old-fashioned carriage. Little Abby just stood there, silent and rooted, in her brown shoes, so incongruous with the pale pink dress that hung straight from her soft baby shoulders. She really *is* adorable, thought Liza. She turned to Evvy, leaving Mrs. Clifford trying to force some response out of Abby.

"I have to feed the baby," Evvy said. "You can come if you want."

"Oh, I'd better stay here, keep an eye on Abby."

She sat back, half listening to Julius and Ham talking about college. Ham had finished last year, the year Julius got through law school, then started right in working at the granite quarry. Over Thanksgiving he and Evvy got married. Liza tried to imagine how it would be if she and Julius had to live with Minx. I would have to turn into a different person, she decided, sighing with relief.

She walked over to the piano, where Derek stood, turning the ice cubes around in his glass with his finger. How can he be so incredibly good-looking, she wondered, when he also looks so much like Ham and their father?

"How about you?" Liza asked. "What do you do?"

"I don't know. I just got out of MIT, but I seem to be going back in the fall for a Master's. Then I guess I'll follow the party line — Clifford Granite."

"You don't sound very happy about it."

"I don't have much say in it." He jabbed his cigarette in the direction of his father. Then he looked at Liza. "What's it like for you, this town?" His voice was gentle. "The back side of the moon?"

Liza smiled. "We've been here a whole year. I'm starting to like it."

"Come on, chicks, time for us to go home." Minx rounded up her brood as if it were her party. Mr. Clifford struggled to his feet.

"Give us a ring whenever you're in town," he boomed. "We could always use a little life around here, pretty gal like you." Liza had never thought of Minx as a gal.

Ham led them out past the gun cabinet in the hall. "Father collects old guns. New ones, too."

"Let's get together," Evvy said to Liza in farewell.

"Finally some people in this town who speak our language!" Julius was talking to Liza the next evening. Minx had gone back to New York. At last. That's how it felt to Liza, even though she had only been there for two days and nights.

"Well, what about Tom and Billie Ray?"

"Oh sure, he's a lawyer, and he's bright and all, but — you know what I mean. And she's from the South."

"I don't think I'm much like Evvy, just because we went to the same college. And you don't hunt and fish all the time like those Cliffords. Anyway, I thought you'd switched from being a Republican."

"Don't be obtuse, Liza. Republican's got nothing to do with it. It looked to me as if you were having a pretty good time up there yourself."

Martinis

AFTER MINX'S visit was finally over, Liza was remembering the first time she had met Julius's mother. Minx was still married to Gubby then, the stepfather nobody liked. Liza and Julius had just driven down from Cambridge to New York City in Julius's gray Oldsmobile. Liza had loved the fact that he had an Oldsmobile. It seemed like such a middle-aged car, not what a college senior would have, if he had *any* car. Liza's father hadn't even worked up to an Oldsmobile yet. But that was before she and Julius were married, before Julius decided cheap (their Henry J) was better.

When they'd pulled up in front of Minx's building on Fifth Avenue, Julius just handed the keys to the doorman, while the other doormen carried their bags into the elevator. When they got out they were right in Minx's apartment.

"We're here," Julius called.

"Yoo-hoo." They heard a husky feminine voice. "Come on in."

Anton, who wore a white coat, took their suitcases. A butler? Liza had never seen a live butler before.

They walked down a long dark hall toward the light. Liza's shoes clicked on the polished parquet floor. Julius's thick rubber soles squeaked.

The room was big and bright, with flowered rugs. Liza was blinded by the light. They were up very high, above all the roofs around them. Late afternoon sunlight streamed through long windows. The room shone with a lot of sparkle: scrolly gold picture frames, light bouncing off the glass, mirrors, shiny floors and furniture, little silver boxes, candle sticks on the mantel with twinkly glass prisms that tinkled like distant bells as Julius and Liza moved through the room.

Minx was clambering to her feet from the corner of a white sofa. One claw-like hand, beringed and scarlet-tipped, held a lighted cigarette in a glass holder. She was so small! Liza had expected someone tall like Julius. Instead, here was someone far smaller than Liza herself. But formidable, that was clear. Minx was wearing a narrow pencil-yellow dress and strappy high heels. Her hair shone like silver. Jewelry at her neck and her wrists —gold and maybe diamonds — glinted in the sun as she stood and came toward them.

"Hi sweetie." She put her bony brown arms around Julius at the level of his chest. "You look exhausted," Minx said in the low level voice Liza was to know so well. Then she held a hand out to Liza. The hand felt like a pretzel, as though it might break if Liza squeezed.

"You're Liza, I know. You look just the way I expected."

Liza was not sure what that meant, but it didn't feel like a compliment. Then for a quick second, Minx wrapped her arms around Liza; Liza was afraid the cigarette would catch her hair. On the table next to where Minx had been sitting, the sun sparkled off a glass half filled with clear liquid.

There was a man in the room, too, who had risen from his chair. He was tall and lean, taller even than Julius, with a head that looked too small for the rest of him, dark hair flecked with silver. He moved smoothly, slowly, like an athlete.

"Hi Lambie," Julius said as they shook hands.

"Hello, my dear, welcome to the big city," drawled Lambie as he grasped Liza's hand. She called him "Mr. Lambert," but no, all three of them told her fiercely, Liza must call him Lambie, too.

"He's an old family friend, darling," Minx said in explanation.

"What can I fix you two?' Lambie asked. "I bet you're ready for a mart, Jules."

"I'll do it, Lambie," Julius said. Well, good for Julius, taking charge, Liza thought. After all he does belong here.

"Where's Gub?" Julius asked, as if he'd read Liza's mind. Inside the silver shaker ice cubes rattled as he shook it.

"Oh Gub's in London," Minx said, waving her cigarette and looking at the ceiling. "Trying to work out one of his deals."

Julius and Lambie both gave short snorts of laughter.

Julius had put a glass beside Liza. She held it, seeing the light through it, contemplating a small white onion in the bottom. It looked like a slug. She took a sip. Horrible, horrible on her tongue. She almost gagged, had to pretend, but of course they'd notice. No potted palms here.

Then Minx said, "You poor darling, no one's even shown you your room! You must be dead after that drive, and I know you're dying to get changed for dinner."

Minx tottered down the hall with Liza, their shoes click-clicking on the floor, Minx's to a faster beat. In her mind Liza ran through the clothes in her suitcase, wondering what on earth she could put on for dinner. She was already wearing her new green suit and her pearls, the best things she had.

Liza had ended up just taking off her suit jacket and putting on a different blouse. White, she remembered now, with ruffles at her wrists: too prim. She winced at the thought of how young and naive she must have looked to Minx and Lambie.

"I THINK you should wear white, Liza." She and Julius had been invited to come for Sunday afternoon tennis at the Cliffords' court. Liza was wearing a white shirt, but she had on her favorite yellow shorts. Julius was white, white, white. Liza had seen him cleaning his tennis shoes. Even Abby was in white, a pique sundress that bared her little soft shoulders, and a white, floppy-brimmed sun hat.

"I probably won't even play," Liza said, as she climbed the stairs to change her shorts.

The Cliffords' driveway was full of cars. "Do you think we'll know anyone?" Liza wondered aloud.

Julius rang the big cowbell by the kitchen door, but, after a few minutes when no one came, they walked in, calling softly. "Hello . . . anybody home?"

They walked through the rooms toward the sound of voices and the intermittent thunk of tennis balls. The french doors from the big living room were open. The court was around a corner from the house, down a shady green path. Liza longed to explore other paths, the whole green garden. She could see a foursome on the court as they got closer, Evvy and Ham playing another couple, all in snowy white. Evvy was wearing a serious-looking green visor.

"Oh hi, darlings." Mrs. Clifford took Liza's hands in hers. "You probably don't know a soul!"

That was true. Mrs. Clifford wore a flowery pink shift. She introduced Liza and Julius as "this nice new young couple" to six or seven people seated along a bench or on the grass. She led Abby over to the sandbox and a cluster of other children.

Everyone was laughing and talking, half watching the tennis. The women looked definitely over thirty, Liza decided. The men didn't look old, but the one called Pete had a stomach that overhung his white Bermuda shorts. "Cigarette, Julius?" he said. Julius, who almost never smoked, took it.

"We don't worry about bothering the tennis players, do we, Ham?" screamed a cushioned blonde. Ham, who was serving, frowned. "I'm Portia Poole, Pete's wife," she confided to Liza, tossing her hair off her face. "You must be so confused — Great shot, Evvy!" she called.

"We're all cousins," another woman said. "Or kissing cousins, anyhow." Her name was Angie something. Angie had the darkest tan Liza had ever seen — on a white person. Angie and Portia had shrill voices, just like Mrs. Clifford's. The men, the husbands, had deep, businessmen's voices; their bass laughter sounded serious, somehow.

"Set point," Ham called, and everyone focused on the game for a second.

Leaving the court, the four players shook hands solemnly. Then the man Liza didn't know yet jumped the net, but clumsily, and everyone laughed. "Atta boy, Miguel — you show 'em."

The pair who walked off the court with Ham and Evvy looked different from the others, smiling and radiant. Liza was sure they weren't married — at least not to each other. The man had an accent — French, Liza thought.

The woman struck Liza as truly glamorous, in a snug white tennis dress with a flippy skirt, and the longest honey-tan legs. Her dark hair was drawn back, confined by a red scarf. Golden hoops dangled from her ears. That is how I'd like to look, thought Liza. She felt inspired.

"This is Valerie, *another* Clifford cousin." Mrs. Clifford introduced the new pair to Liza and Julius.

Valerie's voice was musical, fluty, not shrill like the others. Miguel, tall and slim, leaned over to press his lips to Liza's hand. He was not French, it turned out, but Portuguese.

Ham was explaining earnestly to Julius, "You must have seen those Portuguese paving blocks? They're all over Europe, courtyards and so forth. But they haven't caught on here yet. Miguel's over for a while, helping us develop a market. New product for Clifford Granite."

"OK gang, time for some *serious* tennis," someone said. "Time for some men's doubles. Come on Julius, how about it?"

Evvy drank from the hose spigot and plunked herself down on the grass beside Liza, at one end of the group. She was hot. "We should have won, dammit. E, honey, come see Momma." E, it seemed, was what they called the little boy. He trundled over for a quick hug, his shorts sagging below his knees, and then back to the other children.

"Derek's not here?" Liza asked.

"Oh, he's around. You never know with Derek, what he's up to." Evvy didn't sound as if she cared. "But he hates tennis, that's for sure. The whole scene."

"And Mr. Clifford?" Liza was aware of the absence of those two who had loomed so large at her one and only previous visit here.

"Shh. He's off with Stella. As usual." Evvy spoke in a low voice, close to Liza's ear. The other women were whooping and shrieking. "Everyone knows he doesn't *just* go to fish. Good thing for him that Ma doesn't go in for any of that outdoor stuff." Ma was what Evvy called her mother-in-law.

"What about you?" Liza wondered.

"So why do you think I go along all the time? I used to be scared of guns, scared of heights, bored with fishing. But, no more, that's for sure. I'm a really good shot now . . ."

"Does Mr. Clifford mind you coming — I mean, you knowing about —?"

"Nah, he's used to it. I'd never just want to stay home with E." Evvy made a gagging sound. "And besides! Gotta keep an eye on Ham." She laughed. "Just kidding." But Liza could tell she wasn't.

"Come on, Evvy," Portia called. "Let's get the drinks."

In a few minutes they were back, with an ice bucket, paper cups, and two big glass pitchers.

"Lemonade, kids," Evvy called. They came running, pushing, grabbing. Abby was the youngest. Her face was pink, and her forehead damp. Liza smoothed little curling blonde tendrils off her face.

"*And* sangria for the grown-ups," boomed Pete, stamping out his cigarette on the grass. The sangria was reddish and sweet, with floating slices of orange. Liza had never tasted it before, and wondered if it were potent.

"Save some for us," someone called from the court.

"Plenty more where that came from." Angie poured herself a refill.

"It's one of our little traditions," Mrs. Clifford told Liza, who had already decided there were a lot of traditions. She was trying to learn them as fast as she could.

Liza wanted to ask about Valerie and Miguel, now on the grass, apart from the others. They were talking animatedly to each other, Valerie leaning back on her slender arms, earrings flashing in the sun, one knee bent up, and the other long leg stretched out in front of her. Miguel lay on his stomach, chin propped on his hands, looking up at Valerie. Liza longed to be Valerie, just then.

"Those children haven't even been to the tree house," Mrs. Clifford said. "Come on, E," she called. "Susie, Bob — Pammy, take Abby's hand. Let's show her our surprise . . ."

Liza followed, too, back toward the house and the long green panel of grass that stretched behind it. Halfway down the lawn, on one side, the broad dark canopy of a tree extended over the grass. Its big leaves were deep green, its gnarled trunk black and stout. As she and Mrs. Clifford walked toward the tree, the children scampering ahead, Liza could see stairs winding up around the trunk — not steps, but real stairs with a railing, exactly what you might find in a house. The children dashed up to a solid platform, just over Liza's head.

"It's magical," Liza said. "I always used to dream about a tree house like this." She walked up, running her hand along the smooth railing that ran all around the tree house. No one could fall. There was a table, tiny chairs, and dishes. Abby sat there, clutching someone's stuffed dog, beaming. "Come, Liza," Mrs. Clifford said. "We'll get them cookies and juice. Pam, keep an eye on Abby."

Liza thought she had found paradise. She wanted to wander through this whole enchanted garden to which no one else seemed to give a thought. But, bursting with questions, she followed Mrs. Clifford to the house.

"I love your garden," Liza said. "Who . . . um . . . when . . . ?" she fumbled.

But Mrs. Clifford just laughed. "We had a wonderful Italian man here — in the twenties, it was. Mr. Innocenti, terribly good-looking. We just said, 'Go ahead, Innocenti. Make it beautiful, make it special, do what you want.' And he did — except for the tree house; that had to wait till the tree was big enough."

But Liza had other questions, too. "Does Valerie live near you? She's not, um, married?"

"Oh, no, no. Our lovely Valerie. She *was* married— when she was much too young. A disaster. Here's a plate for the cookies."

"And Miguel? Is he here for long?"

"We've had Miguel since — let's see, skiing season, anyhow. But he'll have to get back sometime. He has a wife and four babies in Lisbon."

Arranging Oreos on the plate, Liza bent over so that Mrs. Clifford wouldn't see her blush. Liza was shocked.

On their way back to the tree house, bearing treats for the children, Liza said, "Mrs. Clifford, would you mind if I walked around the garden?" Liza gazed down an alluring path, densely covered in clipped green, a tunnel of mystery with no end in sight.

"Of course not, dear, go ahead. There's a lot to see. You'll probably run across Derek."

Abby's eyes grew big when she realized that Liza was going without her. Just as Abby's face began to crumple, Mrs. Clifford scooped her up and held a cookie to her open mouth.

Raspberries

LIZA HEARD her own feet scrunch scrunch on the soft packed gravel of the shaded path that ran beneath the clipped trees, straight into the green distance. Faster and faster went her feet. She felt weak with excitement and anticipation. This was magic and she was alone. The path led toward a wall of dense hemlock. Through a gap in the hedge another path angled off in two directions. To her left, Liza could see a statue, a pallid indistinct figure against the dark green. As she drew near, the statue moved. Derek stood up. He'd been sitting on a wooden bench, reading a book. Liza was startled. No longer did she have all this to herself.

"Oh . . ." But after all, he lives here, she thought.

"Liza," he said, as if he'd expected her.

"I was just . . . exploring. I've never seen a place like this."

"This place is falling apart. There used to be three gardeners. Now look at it . . ." Derek brushed his long pale fingers across the wall of green. Liza couldn't understand what he was talking about.

"Now we only have old Leon, and he's such a slob, waddles around with his shoelaces trailing."

"You must have a dovecote somewhere. Le Pigeonnier?"

"No, that would be too logical for Ma. Ugh, it's embarrassing."

Walking slowly, they came to a garden of curious herbs — gray, green, and golden, planted and trimmed into interlacing ribbons, looped and curled, crisscrossed and scrolled, bound about with a miniature hedge of so dark a green that it was nearly black. Just then the sun shone through, sparkling on the dust motes that floated above the herbs. The air was redolent with sweetness, and abuzz with the

71

humming of bees. Liza didn't want to move. She sat down on a bench. Derek dropped down beside her. Liza eyed his dark blue book.

"What were you reading?"

"'For I have known them all already, known them all:
Have known the evenings, mornings, afternoons,
I have measured out my life with coffee spoons; . . .'"

"I remember in English 204 my friends and I used to laugh because T. S. Eliot was so gloomy," Liza said. "'J. Alfred Prufrock.' But . . . do you *like* it?"

Derek replied by quoting another line: "'In the room the women come and go, talking of Michelangelo.' The women around here have probably never heard of Michelangelo."

Liza turned to look at him, his sharp profile, downcast eyes, white shirt with the cuffs rolled back, exposing pale blue-veined wrists. His bare ankles looked fragile and vulnerable; his narrow brown loafers were filmed in dust.

"Is there more to see?" Liza rose quickly and walked on.

They entered a sunny golden orchard, fragrant with ripening apples and grapes, and louder with the insect buzz. Derek drew Liza toward the rows of yellow-leaved raspberry canes, loaded with translucent berries. Even the ground beneath was dotted red with fallen fruit.

"You'd think someone would pick them,"Derek murmured

"Why not you?" Liza was impatient with Derek's complaints. "Actually, I never knew raspberries came in the fall, too."

"If we had a basket." Derek's voice was low. "Here." He held a berry up to Liza's lips.

She crushed its sweetness against her teeth. "Umm . . . heaven . . ."

He fed her one berry after another. Liza laughed until she couldn't eat any more.

"Your lips are stained red. And your tongue." Derek was smiling.

Liza made a face, pouting out her stained lips as if to kiss him, and then whirled away, still laughing. Derek held out an arm to catch her.

"Liza!" She heard Julius's familiar voice in the distance.

"Oh, I've got to go! How do I get out of here?"

Derek pointed with a hand that still held a raspberry. Liza ran, back to Julius, back to Abby, back to real life.

"I didn't know where you'd gone! Abby's got a splinter, and everyone's leaving. You can't just go off like that, no one else does. And you look so wild. Come on."

Early Frost

LIZA HAD been thinking lately that she should try to re-kindle the romance in her and Julius's marriage. Now that they were all settled in their own house, with Julius commuting into Boston every day, things had begun to seem sort of routine. Boring, actually, although Liza knew that was too extreme; she didn't want to think that.

One night when Julius didn't have a meeting, she decided to surprise him. He was downstairs paying bills. She poked around in the back of the closet, and pulled out the sheer, lace-trimmed ivory negligée that had been part of her trousseau. It used to have a matching nightgown, and she'd always worn both parts together when they were first married. Together they were not sheer; you could have even had breakfast in them, though Liza never had.

In the bathroom, Liza fluffed White Shoulders bath powder all over herself, and then put on the negligee, leaving it half open below her throat. She turned out the lights in their bedroom, all except one little lamp on her dressing table. She put her glasses on the bedside table, next to her book. She piled up the pillows on the bed and lay back. When she took off her velvet headband her hair slid down one side of her face, like a movie star's.

She tried different ways of lying, thinking of those pin-up pictures of Rita Hayworth and Betty Grable. During the war, when Liza was still in school, she'd read how all the soldiers had them in their barracks — to remind them of home, or something.

She tried putting one arm behind her head, and then the other. She crossed her feet; then she tried putting one knee up. It was best if the knee was up just a little bit. She fixed the negligee so it covered most of her — but you could still see through it. Then she decided to open the top a little, especially on one side, so it looked as if it were accidental. She thought the effect was about right.

Julius should be coming up soon; it was about time. Liza's elbow was getting stiff, up by her head, and she wished she could read some of her Graham Greene, *The End of the Affair*. She was just at a good part.

She put one knee down, and the other one up. Finally she heard Julius's slow tread on the stairs. All the floors in their house creaked.

He was holding his suit jacket when he came into the room. The top button of his shirt was open, under his tie.

He stared at Liza. She'd thought maybe he would lunge at her like a hungry tiger, maddened with desire. But Julius just looked sort of pained, turned, and hung up his clothes in the closet.

After he turned out the light, he climbed into his side of the bed, under the covers. He reached an arm over, and patted Liza twice on the shoulder. She lay rigid.

"I went out to cover the tomatoes," he said. "We may get a frost." Julius yawned. "Maybe you should get out our electric blanket tomorrow . . ."

Liza felt as if she were already frozen. After a while she got up, and put on her flannel nightgown and a pair of clean white socks. If her feet were cold, she generally felt cold all over.

Wallpaper

BILLIE RAY Ryan was coming to help Liza hang wallpaper in Abby's room. Julius was taking Abby's crib apart so they could move her to another room temporarily.

Abby cried when she saw her bed collapsing. "Oh, Abby," Julius snapped. "Don't be a silly. You're going to have the best room in the house . . . damn it, where's that other washer? Why do they make these stupid things so impossible?"

"Take it easy, Julius — you're not setting a very good example."

"Example of what, goddamn it? You almost made me swallow this screw."

Liza had invited Billie and Tom for dinner. She and Billie would hang wallpaper after dinner.

"Strictly informal," Liza told Billie. "We'll be wearing our work clothes, and dinner won't be anything fancy."

Liza made a casserole ahead of time, something she called goulash. Usually everyone liked it; you just browned the hamburger, cooked up some macaroni elbows, and then mixed it all together with some onion powder and a can of tomatoes. That, plus garlic bread and a salad. Really easy, even though the only lettuce you could get at the Atomic Super Market was iceberg. For dessert they'd have ice cream with frozen strawberries on top. She set the table in the kitchen with some yellow striped placemats made by blind people, a wedding present from her college roommate.

Liza was wearing her levis, plus a frayed blue shirt of Julius's. Billie looked just like always, in a long dress, her sleeveless coat billowing over it. She'd brought them a loaf of her homemade bread. The men were still wearing their lawyer suits. Julius fixed Bourbon Old-Fashioneds for himself and Tom.

"I'll have a Pepsicola, please," Billie said. Liza passed her own special Party-Mix; she'd added raisins to the recipe on the cereal box.

"Have you met the Cliffords yet?" asked Julius. "Clifford Granite; big yellow house up in the Center. Le Pigeonnier." Liza could tell Julius was pleased when it turned out that the Ryans had not. Julius liked to be first.

"What was that about pigeons?" asked Tom.

"That's just the name of their place," Julius said, airily. "We had drinks there a couple of weeks ago, and then they asked us up for tennis last Sunday."

"Oh, tennis." Tom yawned and stretched out his legs. "That figures."

"I don't play tennis myself," Billie said. "But I've seen their sign, the Pigeon-ary. I thought it was an inn." Liza tried to picture Billie in shorts or a skimpy white dress.

"Well," Julius went on. "What I started to say was, the Cliffords are building a bomb shelter out behind their house. They're planning to stock it with canned food, bottles of water, flashlights, candles, a battery radio — everything."

"That's so dumb," Tom said. "Do they really think they could live there? And for how long? If my family was shut up like that we'd kill each other within two days."

"That's no way to live!" Billie said. "And what would they do when the neighbors came rapping on the door?"

"We'd all be dead," said Liza.

"Arrogant snobs," Tom said. "Do you think they'd let any of their workers set foot in their precious little bunker?"

"Well, why should . . .?"

Tom cut Julius off. "I heard they threw a big corporate *fit* when their stonecutters petitioned for a few basic safety measures. Those guys are probably all half sick anyhow from inhaling rock dust. Not to mention losing maybe a hand from some 'minor' slip-up!"

"You're pretty hard on the Cliffords, Tom; they're not that bad. And no one has to work for them."

"Tom, for heaven's sake. Be nice," Billie said. "Let me help, Liza. Dessert time!"

When Liza and Billie had cleared the table, Billie said, "You men are going to do these dishes; Liza and I've got work upstairs!"

"Uh-oh, here we go," Julius said. Tom tied Liza's flowered apron around himself, clowning and simpering.

Liza and Billie walked out, smirking and rolling their eyes.

Billie mixed up the wallpaper paste in the bathroom; she knew just how thick it was supposed to be. Liza set up the Ryans' card table next to hers, and spread newspapers over the top. Billie had brought along her big paste brush, plus the long brush you used to smooth out wrinkles. Liza had her big sewing shears.

"First you have to trim off the edges," Billie said. They both sat there, cutting and talking. The trimming took a long time.

"I love this pattern,"Billie said. "Just right for a little girl." The paper had rows of pink rosebuds separated by blue stripes. "I bet you're hoping for another baby soon. If you don't mind me saying."

Liza did mind. She felt her face grow warm, but they were both looking at the wallpaper in their laps, not at each other. Corkscrews of paper fell from their hands. Their scissors clicked in the silence.

Liza had never talked to anyone about it before. "Every time I talk to Julius's mother she says, 'When? When?' Julius has started saying it too . . . and of course I say it to myself. I feel like such a failure!"

"Liza, honey, you mustn't feel bad. It'll happen, I know, just as soon as you stop worrying. You wait and see. Have you talked to the doctor?"

"I wasn't going to, but he brought it up! He talked about me going to a *specialist*. They have some new pills, blow air into you, make you take your temperature all the time . . . do I have to do all that stuff? And, oh . . ." Liza felt tears come. "Abby's not even two yet. I used to think Oh! Is that really all there is — having babies?" She lifted her head and looked at her new friend. Billie shook her head sadly, and Liza knew the answer was yes.

"But don't worry, Liza sweetie; it'll work out, I know it will. If you hang around me — well, it might be catching. I think I might be pregnant again . . . don't say anything." Billie's smooth face, bent over her scissors, wore a Mona Lisa smile. Liza pushed her hands against her own stomach, hollow as a cave.

They had finished the trimming. Starting in one corner of the room, Billie put up the first strip, showing Liza how to measure and fit the paper smoothly in place. They worked around the room, saving the little odd places over the doors until the end. They were more than half finished when Tom and Julius came to look.

"Honey, we gotta go home!" Tom said.

"I can finish up tomorrow," Liza said. "Billie's a great teacher."

"What about those bubbles?" Julius pointed.

Billie swatted the bubbles with the smoothing brush. "You won't even see them when it's dry."

It was late for a week night, but Liza couldn't get to sleep. Julius's breathing was loud. Liza tiptoed in to make sure Abby was covered up. Then she went into the bathroom and spread a towel over the closed lid of the toilet. She put on her glasses and opened her book where the marker was. John Cheever stories; she was on the third. She was unable to read, though, because tears kept getting in the way.

A Sensible Dog

"JULIUS, DO you think we ought to get a dog? Now that we're living in the country?" Liza had a feeling that Julius was afraid of dogs. He'd grown up in a New York apartment; they'd never had dogs because Julius was supposed to be allergic. Liza remembered how upset he had been by the neighborhood dogs on his walk for the Heart Fund.

They were sitting in the sun on their big granite doorstep, with coffee and the spread-out sections of the Sunday *Times*. Tow-headed Abby, in her blue corduroy overalls and a Fair Isle sweater, was trying to pull Dolly and Kind Dog in her wooden wagon. Dolly kept falling out on the grass, but Abby just picked her up and tucked her back in.

Julius kept reading "The News of the Week." Liza continued. "I think it would be good for Abby to get used to real dogs. And also . . ." She hesitated. ". . . a dog might be protection against — you know, robbers, whatever, while you're at work."

Julius finally looked up. "Is that what you'd like? It would have to be on a trial basis, you know. See if I'm still allergic."

He thought they should get a dog that wouldn't grow too big. "I think a Scottie would be good. Uncle Teddy and Aunt Olive used to have a Scottie. He was called Blackie. A sensible dog." Julius looked pensive.

Liza scanned that very *Times* for the names of breeders.

"I don't believe it! Here's a Scottie breeder right in Bedford. Shall I call?"

Bedford was only ten miles away. The woman who answered the phone said yes, they just happened to have a litter with three males as yet unsold. "A male would be best," Julius told Liza.

The next Saturday they drove to Bedford to see the puppies. The new white ranch house had a perfect lawn and no sign of dogs. Liza pressed the door chime.

"Come right in," said the grandmotherly woman who opened the door. "I'll let my daughter know you're here. Aren't you a little sweetheart." She bent down to leer at Abby, who flinched and leaned against Liza.

Julius and Liza sat on either end of a pale pink velvet sofa. Liza studied the white wall-to-wall carpet. She couldn't hear any dogs. She looked at the knick-knacks on the mirror-topped coffee table — dog figurines, glass and china. No one spoke. Liza gave Abby a red lollypop. Soon Abby dropped the wet lollypop on the white rug. Julius grabbed it.

They jumped up when they heard someone coming to the door. A woman marched in, her hand out to shake theirs.

"You must be the Prescotts. Erlene Block here. Please sit down." Erlene Block had a firm voice, and was wearing a semi-military — or possibly a semi-Girl Scout — uniform.

"I understand you're interested in a Block Scottish Terrier. You must realize it's quite a responsibility."

Julius made a strange noise in his throat. "We just want to get a dog."

"We have lots of space for a dog to run around," Liza said.

Erlene Block frowned. "Run? Our terriers never run loose. Our dogs are confined at all times."

Erlene Block had a list of questions for them. At their responses, she'd bite her lip, or frown, or just look quizzical. Liza had the feeling she and Julius were not measuring up. Julius's face was turning pink. Liza hoped he'd control himself.

Finally Erlene Block stood up. "You might like to see our pups, as long as you're here."

They followed her down a hallway, past framed pictures of dogs and closed doors. The last door opened into a room entirely filled with cages of small black dogs. They all burst out barking. One saggy-looking mother had three puppies yipping at her sides.

"That's our bitch, Block's Black Beauty of Bedford." Erlene Block had to yell over the din. She was a good yeller. "Whelped on Labor Day. The pups have been docked, plucked, eared, vaccinated, and registered. They'll be weaned on — let's see — three weeks from yesterday. Had enough?"

The minute the door was shut the barking ceased. At the front door Erlene Block shook hands with Liza and Julius. "Good of you to come," she said, not smiling.

In the driveway Abby began to scream. "Dog! Dog! Abby's dog."

"Oh, Abby, shut up," Julius said. Abby's legs went limp, and Liza had to hoist her, still screaming into the car.

They didn't say much on the way home. Liza had never before seen Julius look the way she felt — as if the air had gone out of him.

"Bitch," he said as they drove into their own driveway. Liza knew he wasn't talking about Scottish terriers.

Julius had assumed they would get a pedigreed dog, if they got a dog at all. But in the end they decided to see what the Animal Rescue League had to offer. It seemed easier, somehow.

"A dog from the pound would probably not be so high-strung." That was Julius's considered opinion.

"Yes, and it might even be grateful to us for giving it a loving home."

There were so many dogs at the pound that Liza felt as if her heart was twisting.

"How can we choose?" She covered her eyes. "I wish we could take them *all* —"

"Liza, be sensible."

She was smitten with a fluffy tan puppy, with a wagging plume of a tail and soulful brown eyes. She turned to Julius, hoping.

"He looks like Justice Holmes," Julius said. "Oliver Wendell Holmes . . ."

"Wendell," Liza crooned, patting the soft, furry, sweet-smelling creature, so warm against her chest. Then Julius held the puppy.

Liza cradled Wendell in her lap on the drive home. When she put him down on their kitchen floor he made a puddle the size of one of Abby's doll plates. "He knows he's home," Liza said.

Abby jumped down from the babysitter's lap.

"Sweetie, this is Wendell. He's come to live with us."

For the next couple of weeks Liza prayed that Julius would not be allergic to Wendell. As it turned out, he wasn't.

EVVY AND Ham Clifford had finally moved into their own house. Liza couldn't wait to see it. Evvy invited her over one afternoon to have tea; their children could play together.

It was a little old house, right near the quarry. To Liza it looked bleak when she drove up, a scruffy lawn and a cracked concrete sidewalk leading to the back door. Behind the house she could see odd hunks of rusty machinery at the edge of the woods.

A tawny spaniel, whining piteously, had its front paws up against the wire fence of its pen. "You can't let him out?" Liza asked.

"Oh no, Jake's a hunting dog; he never comes in the house," Evvy said. "We don't pat him." Liza pulled her hand back quickly from the panting pink tongue, the pleading brown eyes. Abby clung tightly to Liza's leg, warily eyeing Jake and then Evvy.

"Before we moved here they used it for an office," Evvy said. "The company fixed it up for us. I picked out all the wallpaper."

Liza looked around the kitchen. "You don't have a washing machine?"

"No, the well's not good. But I can take laundry up to Ma Clifford's. She doesn't mind."

Liza couldn't understand why the son of the richest family in town had to live in such a slummy-looking place. In answer to her unspoken question Evvy said, "Ham's dad thinks his sons should start at the bottom, the way he did. So . . . we have to live in this dump for a while. Still, we do get a lot of perks."

Evvy carried her baby on her hip while they walked through the rooms. Everything was dark. Not what I'd choose, Liza thought.

"The sofa came from my grandmother's," Evvy said. "It's the original velvet."

To Liza it looked old and shabby, but of course she didn't say that. On one wall a fierce old man in black glared at them from a gold frame. In a glass case with a padlock Liza saw four guns. She stared; guns right next to E's baby rocker and his stuffed bear.

Every room was different, but to Liza they were all cold and cheerless. She couldn't imagine sleeping in Ham's and Evvy's bedroom, with its brown wallpaper, murky oriental rug, and grim four-poster that almost filled the room.

Evvy made tea. "Our water's rusty, but it's safe if you boil it." They both sat on the velvet sofa, balancing thin cups. "These were Gran's." At the table in the kitchen Abby and Evvy's little boy E had orange juice and graham crackers. E. Hampton Clifford III wasn't even a year old, but he was walking. He followed after Abby, who only wanted to stand close to her mother. Liza was trying to hang on to the teacup.

"You really have to be tough with kids," Evvy said. "Not let them get clingy. E doesn't mind when Ham and I go away; he's used to it. We've had sitters at least every other weekend since he was born."

"You *do*? Where do you go?"

"Well, hunting, mostly. We go all over: Delaware, Chincoteague. Ham's father belongs to all these clubs. Tomorrow we're going to a big turkey shoot in Danvers — not real turkeys, but you can win one; Ham got it last year. We're dropping E off at Mrs. Walker's."

"When did you get into hunting, Evvy?" No one in Liza's family hunted; nobody had guns.

"Are you kidding? I couldn't be married to a Clifford and not hunt!"

"Did your father?"

"I never had a father. And Mummy was . . . oh, you don't want to hear. My sister and I lived with our Gran. She was old, the house was old, the maids were old. Mostly we just took care of ourselves."

"Took care of *yourselves*? Two little girls — how old were you?"

"Oh they fed us and all, but every once in a while Marietta — that's my sister — would say, 'I think we should have baths and wash our hair tonight,' or something like that. One time my teacher said, 'Evvy, are you the one who picks out your clothes every day?' I said yes, and she said, 'I thought so.' When my toes hurt so much I almost couldn't walk, Marietta made me tell Gran I needed new shoes."

Abby leaned against Liza's knee. E clung to Abby with both arms. Liza tried to ignore them, have a grown-up conversation.

"So in college, was it love at first sight with Ham?"

"Oh I was in his room at Lowell House almost every afternoon. We were like an old married couple! I was probably the only girl in my dorm who was sleeping with someone — unless they were drunk."

Liza pulled away from Abby to put her cup on the counter, out of harm's way.

"So when did you and Ham get married?"

"Well, I got pregnant, of course. Gran was too old to care, but we decided we might as well get married. Ma Clifford was nice. So that's where we lived, the biggest house in Rock Hill. Ham started at the quarry, and I had E."

"How was Ham's father?" That crude, repellent man, Liza thought.

"His wedding present to me was a shotgun."

"That was a pretty big hint."

Evvy didn't smile. "Yeah. I learned how to shoot, talk to the dog, clean the gun. And I learned how to wring the birds' necks if they weren't dead yet."

"Home now, Mommy?" Abby whispered. E was still trying to pry her away from Liza.

"E, stop hanging onto that poor girl, will you?" Evvy yanked at him. He fell howling onto the rug. "So Liza, next time, how 'bout the story of *your* life?"

What Liza really wanted was to ask Evvy about Derek, but somehow this didn't seem like the right time; it was never the right time. "Oh, my life is dull," she said instead. It truly seemed dull to her then. But safe.

When Julius came in the door that night, Liza, wearing pearls, flung her arms around him, nestling her head against his shoulder.

"What's all this about?" Julius put his briefcase down.

"Hi Abby. Your mommy won't let me take off my coat."

The Fence

"BRAD SAYS sheep are hardly any trouble," Julius said one evening. "And of course the meat is great. I was thinking we should get some sheep. Brad said he could sell us two ewes; luckily he happens to have two extra right now."

Liza felt her insides tighten. All she could think was, another problem. Brad shared an office with Julius. He and his wife lived equally far from Boston, in another direction, nowhere near Rock Hill. It seemed to Liza that Julius was trying to compete with Brad in terms of rural pursuits. "Back to the land," Brad called it, but Liza knew both he and Julius had grown up in Manhattan. So what was "back" about the way they were trying to live? But if Brad said he'd split a cord of firewood by hand, then Julius had to split even more. When Brad boasted about his brussel sprouts, Julius began raising them, too. So now it was sheep. Well, they might look nice, out in the green field.

Julius spent all day Saturday putting metal stakes around the field. Liza was planting daffodil bulbs in her garden.

"Liza!" yelled Julius. "I need you." Liza had to help him unfurl a huge roll of wire fencing, and try to hitch it to tiny hooks on the metal stakes.

Julius was getting cross. "Abby! You're right in the way." The hooks didn't hold very well. Liza wanted to take a break, but they had to finish. They were supposed to pick up the sheep on Sunday.

"God damn it, why don't they make these lousy hooks bigger?"

"Julius. Please don't swear in front of you-know-who."

"Well, if you'd be a little more . . . here, hold this."

They finished the fence on Sunday morning. Julius carried a shiny new galvanized tub to one corner of the field. Liza dragged a hose out, and ran a few inches of water.

"I don't think we should give them too much water. They might fall in and drown," she said.

"Or Abby might," added Julius.

"Don't say that!" Liza shook her fist.

Later, when they got to Brad's house, his wife Chris, dressed in garage mechanic's coveralls, jumped down from a red tractor to say hello. Brad and their two boys came out of the old barn.

"Want to see your new livestock?" Brad asked.

They picked their way through the barn. Liza held Abby's hand so she wouldn't fall through a hole in the floor.

Cawk-cuk-cuk-cuk. Hens were underfoot. Next we'll have hens, thought Liza. There were geese, too, darting around behind the barn. Abby was scared of them; so was Liza.

The lambs were not as cute as Liza had expected. Their fur — their wool, Liza corrected herself — was filthy, not white, or even cream-colored, as she had imagined. It hung in gray, greasy, tangled locks that shook when they ate. The pasture they were in looked like bare brown dirt. She thought, what a nice surprise it would be for their two when they got to their own lush green field. All the sheep — Brad and Chris had seven — huddled by the fence where the two families stood.

Brad picked up Abby and held her over the fence, as if he were going to put her on the back of the big ram. Abby screamed in terror. Brad and Julius laughed, but Julius held and patted her.

"She'll get used to them," Brad said.

Even the ewes had curly horns, which surprised Liza. Chris and their oldest son each pounced on one of the lambs that were destined for Julius and Liza. They dragged the animals by their feet, roughly, it seemed to Liza. Brad almost threw each one into the back of Liza's clean station wagon. Luckily, she'd thought to put down some newspaper.

Brad talked to Julius about grain. "Just a coffeecanful at night, and again in the morning. Make sure they have water. They'll be fine. We've never had any major problems."

Julius wrote out a check. "Make it out to Chris," Brad said. "It's her pin money." Everyone laughed.

Then they were off. Abby sat on Liza's lap, keeping an eye on their sheep over Liza's shoulder. Whenever they moved near the seat, Abby would duck and cover her head.

Julius backed the station wagon up to a gap in the new fence. When he opened the tailgate, the lambs rushed out, almost knocking him over.

"Quick, Liza, we've gotta get the wire hitched up." Pulling together they closed the gap. Abby began to cry. Wendell barked his tiny puppy bark.

"It's all right, sweetie" Julius, sweating and breathing hard, patted Abby's head. "They can't get out now."

The sheep looked more attractive out in the green field. From a distance you couldn't see how filthy they were. Julius fed them before he went off to work the next morning.

"They'll be fine. Don't pay any attention . . . Just do . . . whatever you do."

Liza called Billie Ray to bring her boys over to see the sheep. They came, but there wasn't much to see, really. They went back inside for fig newtons and apple juice.

Billie Ray was finding it hard to get used to Rock Hill. "People here are so snobby. I'm telling you, all they do is look at your clothes. As if everybody could have Grace Kelly's trousseau!"

Liza tried to interrupt. "But *their* clothes aren't so . . ."

"Oh, Liza they wouldn't snoot you, not with your figure. But back home is so different. In West Virginia everyone knows everyone; you aren't just left alone all the time. Mama would call up Aunt Shorty, or Cousin Hat. You know, if anything happens . . ."

Tom and Billie Ray only had one car, so except for Mondays and Thursdays, when Julius gave Tom a ride to the train, Billie Ray was stuck.

The lambs seemed to be adjusting well. With a little prodding from Julius, Abby named them Sheepie and Lambie. Liza would hear her up in her crib, baa-ing like anything. Liza decided the sheep had Boston accents, with that harsh, flat A sound that in people's voices still sounded alien to her.

On Friday Liza decided to polish the silver. They had a lot of wedding-present silver, and Liza was determined to use it. She liked the look of her mother's tea set on the sideboard. Abby drank milk out of the silver mug that Julius's godmother had given him when he was christened.

Abby was building towers out of soup cans, and Liza was rubbing away with rags from one of Julius's old button-down shirts. The blatting from the sheep seemed louder than ever. This could get on my nerves, Liza thought.

When the baa-ing didn't quiet down at all, Liza thought she'd go and see if the sheep were all right.

It turned out they weren't all right. Sheepie's curly horn was caught in the fence wire. Having already eaten most of the grass in their field, the sheep were trying to get at the grass outside the fence. Liza tried to get the wire off, but Sheepie kept pulling back and twisting her head until she was tangled in strands of wire. Lambie, too, was bleating, looking as concerned as a sheep could, while Wendell barked and ran back and forth. Abby screamed. Liza panicked as Sheepie pulled more and more frantically. The only thing she could think of was to call Julius. He'd have to come home.

Julius was in a meeting, said Miss Peavey, his secretary. Liza told her it was an emergency. She tried to explain what had happened, but Miss Peavey just laughed. Julius sounded annoyed, as if it were Liza's fault, but said he'd be home in an hour and a half, if he could catch the 4:10 train.

Liza and Abby stayed in the house with the windows shut until Julius came. He cut the wire, and called Dr. Russell the vet. Dr. Russell cleaned Sheepie's wounds, gave her a shot, and left some big white pills.

For the next two weeks, Liza had to mash up a pill with a spoonful of grain three times a day, and try to get Sheepie to swallow it. By the third day she felt sick herself every time she had to put her arm around the creature's gray, greasy, woolly neck, wrestle its stubborn black jaws apart, and force open the sour-smelling, greenish-yellow teeth. She raged at Sheepie. "How could you do this to me?" But it wasn't just Sheepie she blamed.

A Day for Dreams

LIZA'S MOTHER had taught her to darn socks. With matching thread you could weave these perfect little patches. It took a while, but was actually sort of fun, once you got into it. The smooth wooden darning egg nestled into your hand, and you felt that you were doing something virtuous.

Liza had all her mother's sewing things, still in her mother's basket. She even used her mother's left-over knitting yarn for mending the socks, yarn ends that her thrifty mother had wound around scraps of heavy paper. Even the paper was reused — old wedding invitations, ". . . immediately following the ceremony," Liza would read, or long-ago Christmas cards, ". . . to you both, Doris and Herb," whoever they were.

One gray drizzly afternoon in November, when she'd put Abby down for her nap, Liza decided to tackle the socks that needed mending. She had quite a pile — all black, all Julius's. He got upset when he'd find a hole in the toe of a sock he was about to put on. Lately he'd get upset because there weren't many socks left in the drawer. "Time to get at it!" Liza told herself.

But it was so quiet. Rain spattered against the window; it was freezing out there. Wendell lay prone on the rug, keeping his brown eyes fixed on Liza. She brought the radio in from the kitchen.

"Life could be a dream. . ." Liza hummed along as she worked. "Sh-boom, sh-boom." She bit the thread off with her teeth.

Yeah, she thought, life could be a dream. Was this it? She had everything she'd dreamed of: a handsome, smart husband, a perfect house, the most precious child in all the world . . . a car so I'm not stuck, a dog named Wendell, finally some friends in Rock Hill. She ought to be happy. She *was* happy, she told herself. So why do I keep seeing Derek when my eyes are shut? How come I remember every single word he ever said to me? She put another black sock in the "done" pile. Then, knowing perfectly well that Julius would have a fit, she reached for a strand of red yarn to liven up the next black toe.

Would it be icy when Julius drove home? I never used to worry about him, she thought.

Liza thought of the time when she'd first known Julius. She remembered a spring day, coming with him out of Emerson Hall into brilliant sunlight after their medieval history class. They'd walked together through the Yard, all the way to the Johnson Gate. Liza remembered how she used to carry her books on her hip, which her mother always said would make her deformed. She'd been wearing her green plaid skirt that day, the one with the tiny pleats. Where was that skirt, by the way? Maybe it had had moth holes. Liza had stopped taking care of her woollens the way she was supposed to, the way her mother had taught her — airing everything in the sun, then packing it all in those bags with smelly mothballs. Liza stabbed the needle fiercely into another sock — and into her finger. A red drop welled up.

Julius had seemed so sure of himself then, she remembered. As she got to know him, Liza used to think he knew everything. His clothes were just right — leather patches on the elbows of that gray tweed jacket, but the patches seemed to belong there; they weren't just covering up holes, the way it was with her family.

Liza had thought Julius had no holes to cover anywhere. He knew how to put money in the bank, get money out, pay his taxes, take his shiny gray car to have its oil changed. He knew how to take notes in class, how to find a book in the stacks of Widener Library, how to arrange the file cards for his thesis, how to drive to New York, where to stop for the best hamburger and a frappe, how to talk to professors, how to talk to his grandmother's friends, how to order a drink at the Darbury Room, and what drink to order.

He'd seemed to Liza so smooth, so sure, so suave — everything she wasn't. If she followed him around he'd open doors for her; they'd follow a set pattern. She used to say to herself, we won't worry about all the things my mother agonizes over. Moths won't get in. Things will just *happen*. You don't need to be always planning ahead. Liza had hated the way her father insisted on telling everyone the exact minute you had to leave to catch the train. It used to embarrass Liza; it still did. With Julius and his family, it had seemed to her, things like that just happened, and they always happened right.

So then what? It doesn't feel quite that way now, she thought. Julius rushes to catch the 7:48 train; he leaves too late; sometimes he forgets his briefcase, and has to run back to the house for it, elbowing past Liza by the door.

Liza heard Abby calling. She switched off the radio, stuffed the rest of the socks in the basket, and went to take her out of her crib. Abby's face was flushed with pink; her pale baby hair stood up in crooked curls; her face looked soft, as if she'd just come back from a ride on a star. She stood there with her arms wide open, ready to hug. Liza held her for a minute, feeling her warmth, inhaling her baby sweetness.

"STOP WALKING around the room, Liza, you're driving me crazy. Can't you stop fussing with the laundry, for once? Just listen, will you? I'm trying to tell you about this case. Since you asked! No, it's *not* good. It was a decision *res ipsa loquitur*, which means that we have to go back and do an entire review of the torts situation, and *then* go back on appeal. It's even worse than *Knox v. Chatham Board of Health*, much worse. Wendell, cut it out! Bad dog."

It was a little after noon one Saturday. Julius had come back from a trip to Dolan's Hardware. He stopped at the Cox farm on the way home for apples and cider and a wedge of sharp cheese. Now he was sitting at the kitchen table, pawing idly through the mail. Abby, in her high chair, spooned up Vanilla Instant Pudding, smacking her lips. Wendell had his nose on the table, sniffing at the cheese.

"Wendell, sit, dammit. I said, *sit.* So anyhow, it's like starting the whole case all over again, right from scratch, ultra vires, findings of fact, relevant decisions, judicial findings, etcetera, etcetera, ad hominem, ad infinitum. A whole new brief! Now do you understand? I don't think you're even listening. Well, are you ever going to get us something to eat?"

Palace Ballroom Blue

LIZA HAD finally gotten around to painting the front hall. She peeled off the old wallpaper, crowded with quaint Dutch children and windmills. It came off easily, in long strips. She crunched up the Dutch children and stuffed them in the trash.

Now the old plaster walls were going to be white. She cleaned them as well as she could, and went to work with a big brush. She painted as high up as she could, but there was one whole section over the stairs that was way out of reach.

"Daddy's just going to have to do that high part with a ladder," she told Abby, who was sitting on the floor, well away from the paint bucket, watching Liza and playing idly with Dolly and Kind Dog. Wendell, the real dog, with his head on his front paws, was watching, too, from the door of Julius's study. Only his eyes moved.

That weekend Julius groaned and complained, but he brought in the stepladder and did it. "I think it looks OK," he said, wiping his hands afterward.

"It looks just beautiful. Why don't you do the wood-work, too?"

"No, no, you're better at the detail stuff," he said.

Over the next couple of weeks Liza worked away at the the window frame, the doors, the stair rail. She was using Olde Williamsburg colors to go with their old house. For the woodwork she had chosen Palace Ballroom Blue, a faded dusty shade that looked more green than blue to Liza, but its aristocratic lineage — minuets and powdered wigs — pleased her.

Last of all was the floor, wide boards once painted barn red, now spattered with white and the blue that was really green. The new color was Tucker Tavern Tan.

Liza swept and mopped the hall floor, up the stairs and down, but figured the only time she could paint the floor was during Abby's naptime. Abby's room had two doors; one of them opened onto the front hall, so after their peanut butter and jelly lunch, Liza shoved Abby's heavy chest of drawers against that door.

"No, Mommy." Abby was confused.

But Liza pulled down the shades and sang "Tender Shepherd" twice. "Have a good sleep, sweetie," she said, as she slipped out the other door. Thank goodness we have these back stairs, she thought.

She put Wendell outside. "Go and play," she told him.

Tucker Tavern Tan turned out to be more yellowish than she'd expected, but of course the square on the sample card was so small. On hands and knees, with a fat brush, she worked her way across the little upper hall and down the stairs. It was easy. When she was finished, she stamped the cover back on the paint can with her foot. The floor was shiny and flawless, even though the color wasn't quite —

She cleaned her hands and barricaded all the doors that opened onto the hall. Then, hearing nothing from Abby's room, curled up on the sofa with *Modern Woman: The Lost Sex.* Why do I read this? she asked herself; it only makes me feel more guilty for having just one child. But she kept on reading until Wendell started barking and whining. "Oh, all right, you silly dog, come on in."

After he calmed down, Liza heard a funny noise upstairs. She listened at the door of Abby's room, and then went in. The crib was empty, and the chest had been moved just enough to open the other door a few inches. "Abby," she screamed. "How did you do that? Why?"

There was Abby in her undershirt and diaper, a stunned look on her face, barefoot in the middle of the freshly painted floor. "Abby, you bad girl, come back!"

But Abby just stood there, starting to cry, with her thumb in her mouth. Liza in her socks took two steps onto the wet paint to grab the child. The paint was slippery; she almost fell, and right in front of Abby were the steep stairs.

Somehow she got herself and Abby back into the room. The new floor was ruined; Abby's floor was smeared with Tucker Tavern Tan. Wendell walked through the wet smears and left little polka-dotted paw prints all across Abby's room. Liza was crying and shaking. Wendell barked in a frenzy. Abby screamed.

"You bad, bad, *bad* girl. How could you? You're naughty! You've ruined all Mommy's work." Liza plunked Abby down hard in her crib. Then, seeing the tan smears made by Abby's painty feet all over her pink-and-white quilt, Liza sank into the rocking chair with her face in her hands.

By the time darkness fell, Liza had arrived at a superficial peace, but when Julius got home of course she told him everything, getting herself worked up all over again. They all trooped up the back stairs to inspect the damage. To Liza's astonishment, Julius laughed.

"Oh, Liza, Liza, when will you ever learn? I *told* you we should hire someone for a job like this."

He'd never said such a thing; Liza knew he hadn't, but he was laughing, and she didn't have the strength to argue.

Town Election, 1956

"BETTY CROCKER went to Vassar."

"Julius!" Liza said. "How do you know that?"

"Betty Crocker is just a marketing device," said Ham. "Someone's scheme for selling more cake mix."

"Betty Crocker went to Smith," Evvy said.

Ham frowned. With him, that only meant that his brow furrowed and his eyes moved even closer together. He forked up another mouthful of chocolate cake.

The four of them were finishing dinner in Liza and Julius's kitchen. Julius, the good host, opened a pack of Marlboros, shaking one out for Evvy.

Ham preferred his own Luckies. Sitting back, right ankle resting on left knee, he exhaled slowly. "Do you think you'll run again for School Committee, Julius?"

"Oh sure, there's still a lot to do. They don't realize it's the twentieth century — never heard of SATs. I'm the only one on the board who even went to college!"

"Except for Mr. Peters," Evvy said. Mr. Peters was the superintendent.

"Yeah, well — Attleborough Normal — but Ham, how 'bout you? Why don't you run for selectman?"

They all looked at Ham.

"Hmm. Our family has always left that up to the villagers. Ed Wells — he's been on the Board for years — one of our foremen at the quarry."

"Your family runs this town," Evvy said. Ham ignored her, but his frown deepened.

"You could really do a lot for Rock Hill," said Julius. "Someone with brains. We'll help if you run."

Liza heard that "we." And he never even asked me, she thought. Ham would be a terrible selectman! But she kept her mouth shut.

Ham sighed. He lit another Lucky from the one he had. "Not sure what Father would say. If I did it I'd have to win." He looked up.

By the time Ham and Evvy left that evening, it was settled. Ham would run for selectman.

Liza tried to talk to Julius while they got ready for bed. "I honestly don't think Ham would be good," she said. "He's so stiff and snobby."

"Oh, Liza, he's head and shoulders above most people in this town. Don't be so negative."

"It's not that I don't *like* him, but . . ."

"Well, listen, it's settled. It'll be good for Ham, good for the town. And after all, the Cliffords owe something to Rock Hill."

Liza got the feeling that Julius believed, deep down, that Ham's running would also be good for Julius.

A week later, Liza was pushing Abby in her stroller from house to house along their road, collecting signatures to get Ham's name on the ballot. Julius made phone calls to everyone who had done work for them and everyone they knew from the Mr. & Mrs. Club. He and Liza dropped by the Ryans one Sunday afternoon. Tom Ryan was not enthusiastic.

"Ham Clifford is the biggest stuffed shirt I've ever met. Why would you want to turn the town over to him?" He handed Julius a Budweiser.

"Actually, the Cliffords already run the town," Liza said.

"Tom, give Julius a *glass*! Ham Clifford is a college-educated man," said Billie. "Just 'cuz you don't agree with him on everything . . ."

"I don't agree with him on *anything*."

"I don't like his politics either, Tom," Julius said. "But

town government is nonpartisan. You're just supposed to do what's best."

Running for office turned out to be entirely political. Julius found himself acting as Ham's campaign manager, a role that he cherished.

"I told Ham that they really couldn't go skiing *every* weekend, at least this year," Julius said to Liza. "He ought to be visible — show up at the dump, the Atomic Market, the post office, etc."

"But no one's running against him," Liza pointed out.

A week later they heard that Ham did have a rival for the vacancy on the three-member board — and it was a *woman*, the first ever in Rock Hill.

Julius snorted. "Patti Foote! What a joke, the dancing teacher. She doesn't stand a chance against a *Clifford.*"

"I'd never trust anyone named Patti with an 'i' at the end," Liza said. "But still, half the little girls in this town take tap lessons from her."

Julius took to dropping in at Le Pigeonnier almost every evening after he got home from Boston. Ham and Evvy had moved back there temporarily, while his parents were in Antigua.

"I don't know, Liza," Julius said to her one night when he got home from the Cliffords'. "Ham is pretty uptight. His father kids him, but if he doesn't win . . . well, it'd be like missing an easy shot at a partridge, or coming in second in the slalom."

Liza thought. "Do you think we should give a party for him?"

"Yeah. A coffee; good idea. I'll check with Ham tomorrow night."

Liza started planning it in her head, while she got ready for bed.

The next day she saw the first bumper sticker. She couldn't believe her own eyes.

"Foote for Select Woman." Royal blue on white. The two Os in Foote were eyes, glancing left, fringed with royal blue lashes.

Liza told Julius about it as soon as he got home from work.

"Bumper stickers!" he exploded. "No one's ever had bumper stickers in Rock Hill!"

"Especially not with eyelashes," Liza said. Deep down, she thought it was clever, something she would like to have dreamed up.

Julius put down his briefcase. "I've gotta go talk to Ham."

"But what about dinner?" Liza's voice came out like a wail. "I made meatloaf. And mushrooms . . ."

"I'll be back." Julius spun out of the driveway.

Liza called people to invite them to the party. She telephoned their neighbors, she called Mr. LeBlanc, who ran the Atomic Super Market, she called Mr. LaComb who'd pumped out their septic tank, she called Fran Headley the postmistress, and all the couples from the Mr. & Mrs. Club.

"That's very kind of you," said Mr. LaComb. "But you know, I played football with Casey Foote."

Casey Foote ran the funeral parlor in their big Victorian house, the old Bassett place. His wife's dancing school took up the other half of the ground floor, through a side door, of course.

Julius was worried, and rushed around more that ever. He decided they should put an ad in the *Rock Hill Beacon*. Ham frowned a lot and puffed on his Luckies. To tell the truth, Liza thought, Ham didn't really have a very good personality.

The coffee for Ham Clifford was, well, a mixed success. Julius and Liza talked it over at breakfast the next morning.

"I thought at least Fran Headley would come," Liza said. "She told me she'd bring Mr. Headley and a dip, at least for a little while. And they know the Cliffords."

"Liza, everyone knows the Cliffords; that's not the point. I thought Ham gave an excellent speech. Right to the point."

"Of course it was good . . . you wrote it. But maybe . . . do you think it was a little too long?"

"Liza, you don't understand. He had a lot to cover."

"'What's good for Clifford Granite is good for the town.' That's what it sounded like to me."

"But that's reality, Lize. It happens to be true, even though I don't agree with all of his views."

"He did look a little funny standing in front of the Audubon print. The peewees seemed to be flying out of his head." Liza giggled.

"Mmm. That was not good." Julius crunched on his toast. "And it was too bad the Albrights left right in the middle."

"Yeah, you'd think they could have gone quietly. Well, at least there were a few people left at the end."

"Evvy's not much of a mixer, is she? She's a drawback, let's face it."

"Political wives are supposed to keep quiet," Liza said. "Look adoring like Mamie. Or Pat Nixon." She put her head on one side, shut her eyes half way, and simpered at Julius.

Julius held up the newspaper, hiding Liza's face.

Patti Foote won the election as Rock Hill's new selectman. Or select*woman*, as the paper and many townspeople called her, putting the stress on "woman."

Ham and his father (and probably that Stella, thought Liza) went on a big-game safari in Kenya. They decided it was too long to leave E with a sitter, so Evvy had to stay home.

Patti Foote didn't say or do much at selectmen's meetings, they heard. But she seemed nice enough. The only problem came a few months later.

It was reported in the *Beacon* that Casey Foote and Ed Wells, the chairman of the board, had caused a disturbance at two a.m. in the middle of Depot Road. Casey had allegedly jumped out of the hearse, leaving the door open. Ed Wells's pickup was parked across the road, entirely blocking traffic — of which luckily there was none, except for the police cruiser. Ed Wells, wearing a zipper jacket, red striped pajamas and a bloody nose, claimed that Casey had pulled his hair. Casey, who had a black eye, was reported to have had liquor on his breath. "Leave my wife alone, you _____," he was quoted as having said.

No one could have known then that two years later, when Ed Wells's term was up, Patti Foote would submit her resignation, give up her dancing school (boycotted then anyway by irate mothers who had withdrawn their daughters en masse), and leave her husband. She and Ed Wells were later spotted running a T-shirt shop at Hampton Beach.

A book called *Peyton Place* was a bestseller that year. Liza spotted the paperback with its lurid cover at Badger's Pharmacy; it was supposed to be about a small New England town. Liza wondered if it was anything like Rock Hill. She could borrow it from Billie Ray, but then she'd have to hide it. Julius would have a fit if he saw her reading a trashy paperback.

"UNDER ARTICLE 7, Dog Licenses, I have a motion to allo-cate all monies received to the Rock Hill Public Library for the purchase of some new books . . ."

This was the first time Liza had attended the Annual Town meeting. On a Saturday morning in March, she was sitting in a back row at the Town Hall on a folding wooden chair exactly like those she remembered from junior high. As a member of the School Committee, Julius sat up front with the other town dignitaries. Liza's row was mostly women she knew from Mr. & Mrs. She was between Gladys Shoemaker and Peg Reilly. They were both knitting the whole time, as was Bernice further down the row. Liza was conscious of being idle. Clicking away with her powerful fingers and thick needles, Peg was rapidly turning a ball of brown, tan, and orange yarn into a brown, tan, and orange . . . scarf? Or was it a blanket? Anyhow, it was already long enough to cover the whole front of Peg's navy blue skirt, where it fell over her knees. Once when Peg dropped the yarn ball, Liza pounced to retrieve it from beneath the chair of the man in front of her. He turned around and glared at Liza until he recognized her. It was Mr. LaComb who had pumped out their septic tank. He looked different in a tie. Liza waggled her fingers at him, and he nodded.

There was so much to look at around the room that Liza had trouble paying attention to the meeting. She knew the moderator, Ben Cox, who owned the town's biggest apple orchard. Liza looked around the hall for other people she knew, thinking, hoping, Derek might be there.

Ben Cox was up on the stage in front of a lectern, with Alice Parlee shuffling papers at a card table next to him. Alice was Town Clerk. She inherited the job from her husband Charlie after he died falling out of bed. Alice had also inherited his black car, which was pretty old, something like a Model T. Looking at Alice, Liza decided she was probably older than she wanted to be, although you had to hand it to her for her gallant effort to look . . . well, lively. Her hair was blacker than you ever saw in nature, and her black eyelashes were so long they almost touched the pink circles on her cheeks. Today she was wearing beads and a silky salmon-colored outfit with long floppy pants, like fancy pyjamas.

Liza tried to pay attention to what Ben Cox was saying, especially when they got into the school part, because she knew Julius would go over it all with her later. Julius was anxious for the town to support his motion to buy new desks for the first grade. "They still have these old ones with *inkwells,*" he'd told her. "Bolted to the floor!"

"All in favor say 'Aye,'" Ben Cox said in his smooth bass voice. The article passed, to Liza's relief. She looked around the room again. The walls were painted the same boring shade of green as her grandparents' kitchen. At the top of the arch over the stage was a carved medallion, also painted green. Liza tried to make it out. Was it a face? Ben Franklin? Some long-ago town father? Or was it just a bunch of leaves?

Gladys tapped Liza's arm with a knitting needle. At the front of the hall Julius was on his feet. "We need your support to hire a modern language teacher for our youngsters. We're more than halfway through the twentieth century, and it's time to offer our youngsters — *your* youngsters — a language that is not dead."

Liza had never heard Julius use the word "youngsters" before. But, after all, she told herself, he's never been on a school committee before.

Seated against the windows were the police chief's mother and his beautiful new wife. Chief Gerrity's late father had held the post before him (for about forty years), so old Mrs. Gerrity was used to being treated with respect in Rock Hill. Her hands were clasped over the front of the black coat she still wore in mourning for her husband. But Liza could hardly take her eyes off Doris Gerrity, the wife of the new chief and still a bride. From this distance, Doris looked exactly like Jackie Kennedy, the same poufed-out dark hair, little white gloves, and ankles neatly crossed. Her turquoise suit and the matching turquoise pillbox hat plunked onto the back of her head looked exactly like what Jackie would wear. "She must be bored out of her mind," Liza thought, picturing her instead at some Jackie-ish horse show or political tea party. The illusion was shattered as soon as Liza met her afterwards and heard Don's squeaky treble voice in an accent like maybe South Boston, one of those parts of the city where Liza had never been.

"We'll adjourn for a lunch break until 1:15," the moderator was saying. "Our high school youngsters are selling sandwiches and brownies downstairs to raise money for their field trip to Nantasket Beach."

Liza joined Julius at a long table with Superintendent Peters and other town officials. They all ate their tuna sandwiches. "Ham swore he'd be here," Julius complained to Liza. "He should take an interest, even though he lost the election."

There were so many articles that the meeting was still not over by five o'clock. Liza scanned the crowd as they filed out. No Derek. Ben Cox had announced that the meeting would continue on Monday evening, so Liza lined up another sitter.

On Monday it snowed, and was still snowing when Julius drove Liza up to Town Hall again. Liza had brought along a little bag with three of Julius's black socks to be darned. She hoped the knitting women would approve. The crowd was much smaller than on Saturday. Wearing his earnest civic expression, Julius walked up to sit with the town officials.

Now they were voting on the budget for the Cemetery Department, presented by Casey Foote of Foote's Funeral Parlor. "I'm here to ask, ladies and gentlemen, for your support for the town to purchase a lowering device, something we badly need."

"What is a lowering device?" shouted someone.

"It's a mechanical — umh, machine. You rest the casket on it, and then you lower it. Our cemetery crew is, let's face it, getting on in years, and their backs — well —"

Just then the lights went out. Street lights, too. There was a sudden buzz of voices. People rose to their feet, and Liza heard nervous laughter. Julius found his way back to where Liza was sitting. "This is serious." Alice Parlee was the one who produced a candle. She had matches, of course, with her cigarettes, but why a candle? Liza wondered. Chief Gerrity had a powerful flashlight that reflected off his police badge and his brass buttons and his round red face, blinding everyone within range. Ben Cox banged his gavel. "Ladies and gentlemen. Ladies and gentlemen. Please. I need a vote on the lowering device before we adjourn." Bang, bang. People were milling around in the dark, chattering, edging anxiously toward the doors, but there was a resounding "Aye," and no one said "Nay."

Chief Gerrity and his lieutenant shone their flashlights on the stairs, as everyone went cautiously down and out into the snow. There was more light once they got outside. The darkness didn't seem so black. Liza's heart floated up like a birthday balloon when she spotted a familiar face at the bottom of the steps.

"Oh, Derek, hi. Isn't this exciting?" Now the darkness felt warm and romantic. It seemed like a time that might bring people together.

"Hello, Liza'" he said, smiling. "Julius."

All Julius said was "Hi." He took Liza's arm, and led her through a foot of snow to their car. They didn't talk much on the way home.

New Light on the Subject

JULIUS DECIDED they should have their kitchen remodeled. Liza had gotten used to the way it was, although she recognized certain drawbacks. The kitchen wing had been added to their old house by prior owners, the Heathcliffs. Old Mr. Jewkes down the road had told Julius that the Heathcliffs had kept two state wards in the attic to help with the farming. Julius thought the state wards had also built the kitchen in their spare time.

The kitchen's most obvious defect was the shallow step that ran across the middle of the floor, right between the sink and the big iron cookstove. Everyone either tripped over it at first, or fell. Julius's mother Minx had badly bruised both her shins on her first visit. She was mad because she was about to head off to Hobe Sound, and she wanted to look beautiful on the beach. Also, the roof slanted so that half the ceiling was quite low. Julius hit his head nearly every day, either on the ceiling or on the doors. The back door was especially hazardous; while you were reeling from having hit your head, you might fall against the wall of the back entryway, and get stabbed by the nails that held on the asbestos siding. Plus the heating system was not too good. Liza couldn't help being startled on their first really cold morning when she noticed that the water in Wendell's dish beside the stove was frozen solid.

They hired Waldo Croch, a new architect from Cambridge who was recommended by one of the lawyers in Julius's office. When Mr. Croch —"Pliz; call me Valdo." — came to inspect the site, he was wearing thick green corduroy pants and a black shirt printed with big white flowers. Like something at the Museum of Modern Art, Liza thought; she had never seen a man in a shirt like that, or with hair so long. Waldo warned them right away in his heavy German accent, "You must realize I am a Modern Architect."

"Of course," said Julius. "We wouldn't want pseudo-colonial. After all, it's the fifties!"

"Oh I agree," Liza said. Waldo made her feel modern, too. She wouldn't admit that she actually liked colonial, phony or not. She tried to visualize a modernistic wing on their house, but found herself staring at Waldo's orange leather sandals instead.

Liza had to cook on a hotplate during the long months of construction. She carried the dirty dishes upstairs to the bathroom sink. Sometimes she used paper plates, an extravagance that made her feel guilty, not unpleasantly so.

Billie Ray came over to look. Her boys, Thurman and Donny, ran around picking up curly wood shavings. They stuck them in Abby's hair. "Boys, don't you get in the way of the workmen," Billie called.

"How do you like it?" asked Ed the head carpenter. "Real different, anyhow. My wife wouldn't go for it, that's for sure."

Thurman stepped on a nail. Billie hugged and patted him until he stopped screaming. "It's all right, honey, you had your tetanus."

Liza spread out Waldo's plans for Billie, but Billie wouldn't even look. "I could never have Modern," she said. "My crocks, my marble dough tray — it just wouldn't seem right. But you're so young, Liza."

Liza couldn't picture Billie in a modern kitchen, either. For one thing, her mammy clock wouldn't really go. It hung on Billie's kitchen wall, a turbaned Aunt Jemima whose arms told the hours and minutes.

Waldo Croch appeared now and then to check on the construction. Liza never knew when he was coming, so she tried to be prepared all the time, like a Girl Scout. She imagined how the secretaries in his office would dress. Definitely not Peter Pan blouses and knee socks! Liza took to wearing black tights, and no blouse under her sweater. That seemed more . . . continental, she thought. Not that Waldo or anyone else seemed to notice.

Waldo discussed knobs and casings and finish nails with Ed the carpenter. One day he brought a light fixture to show Liza. Stainless steel, shaped like an ice cream cone.

"These we hang on a track, over your head. Shadows; very interesting. Also we have fluorescent. You like fluorescent?" He put his pockmarked face up to hers.

"Well." Liza was unprepared. "They do give sort of a cold light —"

"Ah, yes, clean, fresh, very Nordic."

Liza decided right then that clean, fresh, Nordic light was exactly what she and Julius needed.

One day Waldo walked in just after Liza had put Abby down for her nap. Wendell, who had never accepted Waldo, barked fiercely as usual. "Down, you hound." Waldo flapped a roll of plans in Wendell's face.

"Would you — have you had any lunch?" asked Liza. The carpenters were still eating theirs, out in the truck.

"Ah, thank you, my dear. So kind." While Waldo inspected things, Liza got out some cheese, olives, carrots from Julius's garden. She heated water for tea on the hot plate, and wished she had something more ethnic than Hollywood Bread. She carried a tray out to her garden, where they sat under an apple tree in the warm sun. The few first daffodils had opened, and the ground at the edge of the lawn was blue now, carpeted with scilla, planted by unknown hands, long before Liza was here.

Waldo asked her about herself. "So you have a university degree? And you do nothing with it? Surely that is difficult."

His gaze at Liza was searching, but also, she felt,

sympathetic. Not many men were interested in her mind. Julius didn't really think about other people's minds.

"In Europe is very different. My wife, for example; she is also an architect. She designs furniture."

Liza didn't know what to say. She felt mixed up inside. Before she'd met Julius she used to imagine becoming a career girl in New York after college, working maybe for *Look* magazine. But even before they were married, she'd stopped dreaming of any other life. *This* was her destiny, a husband, a house, a child — even though there should have been four or five children — a dog, a station wagon. She was rattled by Waldo's suggestion that she might not be satisfied. I have everything I want, she told herself. But then — why do I keep thinking about other things? And not only about Derek —

Waldo's eyes were on her. Liza felt herself blushing. She stood up. "Well, I mustn't keep you from your work." She picked up the tray and fled into the house.

The new kitchen had enough cupboards for Liza finally to unpack all her wedding present dishes. It had a cathedral ceiling, and more windows than walls. The sun was so bright and hot even on winter days that Liza sometimes felt dizzy. At night she couldn't tell who might be watching her through the black glass. When she had the windows measured for curtains, Julius was incensed at how much it would cost to cover all the glass with Marimekko cotton.

"That's insane, Liza! You've got to do better than that."

It's not my fault, she told herself; I can make curtains for any normal window, but not these. She was determined, but in the end she decided to leave the back window uncurtained. It seemed unlikely that anyone would spy on them from out there.

Party

WHEN THE new kitchen was finally finished, Julius and Liza gave a party. They invited Tom and Billie Ray, Ham and Evvy Clifford, and a lot of people from the Mr. & Mrs. Club. They'd thought of inviting Waldo Croch, but Julius didn't think he'd fit in.

Liza wore a new dress, very fancy: red dotted Swiss, off the shoulder, with a wide swirling skirt held out by a stiff crinoline. She had to be careful not to knock things off tables when she moved. "Mama pretty," Abby said when Liza tucked her in her crib upstairs before the guests got there.

Liza had set out all their ashtrays. She'd put little silver bowls of salted nuts in strategic spots around the living room. Julius had lined up rows of glasses on one of the new kitchen counters.

"Did you get the olives? The cherries?" She had. She handed Julius each thing as he asked for it, and pointed out the supply of extra ice cubes.

Chipper and Peg Reilly were the first to arrive. Liza saw them walking up the path. Spider and Tilly were right behind them, along with Erford and Mildred Pickens. Spider's brown figured tie came only halfway down his white shirt front. Below that was a vast convex curve that ended finally at the big silver buckle of his belt. The buckle was made up of his initials, ERF. Liza wondered what was his real first name. Maybe Elroy?

He patted Liza on the back, laughing. "Did you know your little girl's up there standing at the window in her birthday suit?"

"Spider!" Tilly said. "Don't make Liza feel bad about the baby." She and Spider had no children. Everyone else was nice about it, but Julius frowned at Liza. She click-

clicked up the stairs in her high-heeled white shoes, thinking Julius was as usual right: she should have lined up a babysitter.

Everyone wanted to see the new kitchen. "It sure is modern," said Chipper, shaking his head. "What do you hide in all those cupboards?"

"I sure wouldn't want to have your heating bills, unh-unh," Erford said.

"Plenty of room for all your preserves, that's for sure," Peg said.

All my preserves? Liza had that sinking feeling. Evvy loved the kitchen. "I envy you." Julius was showing Ham and Chipper the built-in bread drawer and flour bin, and the special cupboard for trays.

"That's pretty ingenious," Chipper exclaimed. "I could do that in a couple of hours in my workshop. And a whole lot cheaper, I'll bet!"

Liza had made a huge casserole of macaroni and cheese, but everything else was cold: ham, Waldorf salad, tomato aspic from her mother's recipe, with cottage cheese in the middle, plus rye bread already buttered. She prayed that she'd fixed enough; all these big men, especially Chipper and Spider. Chipper had on a new emerald green sweater, knitted for him by Peg, with rows of orange trees encircling his chest and back. It made him look huge. After everyone had their drinks Liza stopped worrying.

No one knew Evvy and Ham Clifford very well. None of the Cliffords mixed much in the town, though of course everyone knew who they were. Evvy was talking to the other wives about their children, her little boy, recipes, things like that. Ham, in his double-breasted blue blazer, puffing on a cigarette, looked ill at ease. His craggy face was stiffer than ever, and he jiggled the coins in the pockets of his gray flannels. He didn't seem to be talking to anyone, but he looked as though he'd like to be talking to Tilly, the way he kept staring at her. Liza didn't really think Tilly was Ham's type, with her silvery ankle bracelet and the tight spangly dress that showed off her plump bottom and her much-too-big bosom, only about half of which was covered up. Probably Ham is just remembering Tilly from childhood, Liza thought; after all they both grew up in Rock Hill.

Liza kept passing nuts and chips, and urging everyone to help themselves to more food or another drink. The room was fogged with smoke. Peg Reilly started playing the piano; she was so good it sounded just like a player piano. People gathered around and sang. Peg played "The Skater's Waltz" and "Winter Wonderland," even though it was spring, and "Three Coins in the Fountain."

Two hours later, the ashtrays were overflowing; Liza went around emptying them. Billie Ray Ryan had begun singing, surprising Liza with her mellow, bluesy voice: "— when the lights are low . . ." Liza walked into Julius's study, where the lights were low, stopping when she caught sight of Tom Ryan's back in a corner of the room. He stood with his feet together, legs straight, arms raised, leaning into the corner as if he were doing one of those exercises that are supposed to strengthen your shoulders. But then Liza saw two twinkling white hands on Tom's back, and a pale leg curled close around his. Plump calf, slim ankle, and the high silver heel of a sandal. Tilly. Liza backed quickly out of the room.

Her heart was pounding. Had they seen her? Billie was still singing. She saw Erford Pickens give Peg a little pinch on the bottom. Peg smiled up at him without missing a note. "I hate to see . . . that evenin' sun go down," sang Billie.

Ham and Evvy had to leave. "Great party," Evvy said. Liza was not sure they'd had a very good time.

Then everyone left. Erford couldn't seem to walk very well; Julius had to help him down the path. Chipper howled at the moon. "Ah-oo."

"*Lovely* party," said Peg.

"Tom, we've got to get the sitter home," Billie called.

"Take me home, baby," Tom said, mimicking Billie's voice and southern accent. "Get in the car, you old drunk Yankee," she said.

"Come on, Liza, leave the mess till morning," Julius said, clumping up the stairs. Liza was just going to put the food away, so Wendell and the mice wouldn't get it. A success, she decided. Except for that business of Tom Ryan and *Tilly*. How could he go for her? So cheap. And anyhow it wasn't right, and poor Billie. Liza knew she could never breathe a word about it to Julius; he'd make it all worse. Then Liza thought of Derek. Well, he's in Cambridge, and I'll never . . . . But, oh . . . . Liza ended by cleaning up everything. It was so quiet and peaceful at night.

Billie found out. She didn't tell Liza how she knew, but when she called on Monday, she was crying into the phone. Liza went to see her, even though she didn't want to. They made Duane watch the other children out in the yard.

"What am I going to do, Liza? I trusted him! Now I don't even want to see him, let alone touch him! He tried to make up — and I just pushed him away."

Billie was holding the stub of a Lucky strike; this was the first time Liza had seen her smoke. Out the window the children ran across the patchy grass.

"I feel like I never want to be close to him again." Billie's face crumpled. She dabbed at her pink nose with a Kleenex. "He's just like every other man. Animals!" she sobbed. "And I used to think he was . . . special."

Liza felt like putting her hands over her ears. If it were me, I'd try to hide it, she told herself.

Billie sat up. "Just wait till he comes home, dragging his tail like a mongrel pup. I'll tell him what's what." She pounded out her cigarette against a white ironstone saucer, and took a swig of Pepsicola. The madder Billie got, the more cheerful she sounded.

"Yes," Liza said. "You tell him." She was cheered, too, for the moment.

Driving home, Liza was ashamed that she'd been unable to comfort Billie, but she felt a longing for something to fill a hole in her own life. Then guilt washed in again, guilt at her own transgressions, real and imagined.

"GET RID of Those White Rings!" Liza was leafing through the copy of *Woman's Day* that she'd picked up at the Atomic Super Market. Julius had left for work, and Abby was building a soup can tower on the floor of the new kitchen. Liza was still sitting over the remains of breakfast, sipping cold coffee. Get going, she told herself, not moving. "Next time Hubby lights up a cigar," she read, "save some of the ashes, and . . ."

The phone rang.

"Oh, Evvy, hi . . . I'm just being lazy today. A million things I ought to do, but . . . . No, I never . . . Julius's mother does needlepoint, but I've never tried it."

A week later, Evvy came with E over to Liza's house. Peggy Sue's mother baby-sat for both children while Evvy drove Liza to Pepperell for their first needlepoint lesson, from a woman she'd heard about.

"Would you mind driving just a *little* slower? Sorry to be such a . . ." Liza's knuckles were white.

"I can't stand these women in Rock Hill with their everlasting *knitting*," Evvy said. "Click, click, making everyone else feel guilty."

"And the sweaters they make are mostly so hideous."

"Did you see what's-his-name, Puggy Swenson, in that purple-and-yellow thing?"

"Yeah, yellow *fish*. That's his hobby. I'd really like to be able to make something beautiful . . ." They were passing hills dotted with apple trees, white with bloom now, row on row, as far as Liza could see and up to where the blue began.

"A friend of Ma Clifford's needlepointed a whole stair carpet. Scenes from their married life on each tread."

"You're kidding!" Liza giggled. "Have you seen it?"

"Well, no, but . . ."

"It could be pretty funny. Are they still married? I mean, if you think about it: 'Here are George and I after . . .'"

Evvy didn't seem to be amused. "I might start on chair seats, for our dining room. When we have one. I have eight of Gran's chairs. Chippendale."

Liza began with a footstool in a design of autumn leaves. For Julius, she decided.

Third Man

THE CLIFFORDS were having one of their big parties, the last weekend in June.

"It's a bon voyage party, dear," Mrs. Clifford told Liza on the phone. "For Derek. He's going off to Europe, you know. For the summer, with his Eurailpass. He's been working *so* hard, poor child, I thought he deserved a little break, and Hampton agreed with me, for once. So, we'll see you and that nice husband of yours about eight?"

The living room at Le Pigeonnier was crowded, but no one, as far as Liza could tell, was from the Mr. & Mrs. Club. Most of them probably didn't even live in Rock Hill. This was a different world. She and Julius had already met quite a few of these people, lounging around the Cliffords' tennis court on Sunday afternoons. If the men weren't Clifford cousins and part of the granite company, then they were "in textiles."

Evvy was introducing Liza to a few people she didn't know. "This is Cotton Clifford. Her husband Shep — over there with the mustache — he's the company treasurer."

Cotton was older than Liza and Evvy, in her thirties, Liza thought, like most people at the party. The cleavage at the front of her low-cut white dress was weathered and already tan.

Liza had to shout over the noise of voices and music. "Is your name really Cotton?"

"It sure is! Daddy named me after the goose that laid the family's golden egg, if you know what I mean. I could kill him!"

"I think it's cute," Evvy said.

The women's voices were shrill, punctuated by little screams. A group of men was clustered around the mirrored bar. No one paid any attention to the big nude painting that was supposed to be Mrs. Clifford. A long table at the other end of the room held more bottles. There wasn't any food, just a couple of half-empty bowls of potato chips. Everyone seemed to be laughing. Liza didn't see Mr. or Mrs. Clifford.

The only music you could hear was the piano — the thump thump of the bass. Derek was playing, his cigarette stuck to his lower lip. At either end of the keyboard stood a half-empty glass of whisky. Derek wasn't talking to anyone, just playing. The haunting repetitions of *The Third Man* theme hinted at intrigue. Decadence. Liza stood by the piano, then leaned an elbow on it, cradling her chin in her palm. She watched Derek, his long strong fingers, his bent head. His hair was longer than his brother's; it swung across his forehead in time with the music. Liza hummed along, inaudible even to herself. She felt like Lauren Bacall. Sultry. She wanted to hop up to sit on the piano, but of course she didn't. Derek appeared oblivious. Then his eyes met hers, staying there as he played.

One of the wives came over and shrieked at Derek to play "Deep in the Heart of Texas." "I'm from there, honey," she told Liza. "A long way from home — a *long* way." She laughed, rolling her eyes.

Liza walked off to look for Julius.

She couldn't see him, so she went into other rooms. The pine-panelled library seemed to be empty, until she noticed a silent couple entwined on a sofa. Not Julius. She turned quickly away, appalled that the thought had even crossed her mind. I guess I should be more . . . sophisticated, she told herself.

She saw Derek by the lighted gun cabinet in the hall, glass in hand. Liza paused, suddenly shy.

"Well, hello." A thin smile flickered across his face. "I haven't seen you since . . . last summer, when the raspberries were ripe."

Liza could feel her face turn pink. She didn't look at him. "That was a long time ago."

"Not that long. You haven't forgotten, anyhow."

"No."

"Hasn't anyone given you a drink? Poor little Liza." He ran one finger down her cheek.

She stepped back. "I'm not much of a drinker."

"Here." He held his glass to her lips. Liza smiled and sipped.

"That's enough," she sputtered.

"Come on," he said, holding out his hand.

He led her through the bright kitchen. A man she didn't know was shaking ice cubes into a bucket. The Cliffords' cousin Portia, encased in a tight green dress, was leaning on the counter beside him, giggling. They straightened up.

"Hey Derek. Where you headed?"

Portia's shrill laugh followed Derek and Liza out the back door.

Outside it was quiet. Wispy clouds scudded across an almost-full moon. Black trees loomed above the driveway and the house. The trembling cry of a screech owl sounded from far away. Liza looked at Derek, listening. The moon shone in his eyes. The driveway was filled with empty cars, colorless, hulking night creatures, glowing here and there where the moonlight touched them. Liza hugged her arms.

Derek wrapped his jacket around her shoulders. "Come." They walked around the house. "It's magical outside at night," he said. "Especially when there's moonlight."

"Oh, yes," Liza said. "In summer I always go out at night, before bed. If Julius goes outside he takes a flashlight, but you can see much more without a light."

They walked past the big bright windows of the party room. From outside the scene looked frenzied, cavorting couples, mouths opening, closing. A buzz of meaningless sound came from the open windows.

"A bacchanal," Derek said. They walked to the tennis court.

"It's so bright we could play," Liza said.

"If we had rackets," he said.

"If we had a ball." They smiled.

Liza said, "You almost can't see the stars, it's so bright."

Together they walked through the garden, following the path beneath the long tunnel of clipped greenery. When they came to the tree house, they paused. Fireflies flashed their tiny beacons. The lawn was silver in the moonlight; the tree house was shadowy and dark. They climbed the curving stairs and perched on the railing.

"Are you s-s-still reading T-T-T. S. Eliot?" Liza couldn't stop her voice from shaking.

"Aagh. I wish. But I've had papers, exams. And now I'm off to see the world, or part of it."

"I envy you. You're so lucky."

"It's a great reprieve; I didn't expect it." His tone changed, somber. "Until September. After all, I'm supposed to be the geologist of the family."

"Who says?"

"My father." Derek stood up. "I shouldn't keep you out here. You're cold."

"Listen to the owl." She leaned toward Derek, the smell of cigarettes and some elusive sweetness.

"A screech owl," Derek said. They listened.

"*Two* screech owls." The trembling cry sounded far away.

"They're talking to each other."

Derek put an arm around Liza, light as air on her shoulder. Their heads were together, their two faces tilted toward the moon, listening.

Then they heard it again, that haunting, tremulous sound. Twice. Three times. They kissed, their rough dry lips soft as feathers.

Oh, thought Liza, what am I doing? She pulled back, stood up. "I've got to go in." She ran down the steps. Derek followed her toward the house.

At the door, she turned and handed him his jacket. "Thank you Derek," She couldn't see his face in the shadows.

Liza hurtled through the blinding empty kitchen. The big room was almost black. Ten or a dozen people lay sprawled across the sofas, the stuffed chairs, the rug. All you could see were the glowing scarlet tips of their cigarettes. Coals were still red in the fireplace. From the phonograph the piercing trumpet of Harry James floated thinly on the air — "One O'Clock Jump" — reminding her of every party she'd ever been to. It must be after one o'clock now, she thought, still breathing hard.

Cotton saw her in the doorway.

"Well hello Liza, honey. You're out past your bedtime." The words came out thick.

Liza spun around and walked toward the library. Julius was stretched out in a leather chair, beside another dying fire. He didn't notice her right away. Ham, with his chin in his hands, was talking to him.

"Don't be naive, Julius," Ham frowned. "It's never going to work, all this mixing. Face it, most of them probably don't want it, either. If it weren't for a few loud mouth do-gooders . . ."

Even in her confusion, Liza was sure she knew what would come next. She expected Julius to tell Ham all about the good Negro, the man at his office who had charge of the file room. But Julius only yawned. He saw Liza.

"Look who's come to take me away." He pulled himself up. "Time for beddy-bye, Ham, old scout. Forget about the Commies, at least for tonight."

Liza saw that Julius, who usually kept an eye on her at parties, hadn't given her a thought. She didn't know what this meant, but she didn't care. Julius handed her the car keys. They didn't speak while Liza drove. Their own house seemed so quiet. With Mrs. Brine, Peggy Sue's mother, babysitting overnight, and now asleep in the guestroom,

Liza had one less thing to worry about. The dishwasher was already unloaded. Liza set out cups for their coffee the next morning. As she walked upstairs, she could hear Julius's brown shoes drop to the floor as he took them off. One. Two.

The Virtuous Wife

SUNDAY MORNING, after the Cliffords' party. Liza woke with a start. Her head was full of lively, complicated, crowded dreams that vanished even before she lifted her head off the pillow.

Ten o'clock! How could she have slept so late? The house was quiet. Downstairs, Wendell was lying on the sofa, where he knew he was not supposed to be.

"Wendell! Bad dog." Liza slapped the sofa cushion. She found Julius's note. "Gone with Abby to take Mrs. B. home and get the paper."

While Liza had been lying there in bed, Mrs. B. must have dressed Abby, given her breakfast, done all the things that Liza normally did.

She pulled out cookbooks while she sipped her coffee. Liza usually tried to make an extra-good dinner on Sundays, the way her mother had. Julius appreciated it, she thought. She went over a menu in her head. Let me see, roast chicken, rice, a package of our frozen beans, and . . . what for dessert? She wanted it to be homemade, not just ice cream from the freezer. Think I'll try banana cream pie. Flako pie crust, rolling pin, vanilla pudding mix . . . She saw Julius walking up the path with Abby and put on her apron before she went to meet them.

Later, while the pie was cooling, Liza began hacking away at a pile of rhubarb stalks that Julius had brought in from his garden. She cut the stalks into little pieces. Tough! Or her knife was dull. She hated rhubarb, actually, but you can't waste it. Echoes of her mother and Julius. She piled the fruit into her biggest pot, loaded it with sugar, plunked the pot onto the stove, and began pushing it around with a wooden spoon. Oh, I know, she told herself, I should be making more pies! But I'm not going to; this'll have to do.

127

Liza's mind kept wandering off as she stirred, remembering the night before.

Finally the rhubarb was soft. She spooned the hot purée into little blue boxes for the freezer. Nine boxes, nine meals next winter with rhubarb on the menu. "There," she said aloud to no one.

ONE SUNNY September morning Liza was trying to catch up on all the things that needed to be done. End-of-summer tasks, like putting away their bathing suits, their tennis shorts, and Abby's faded sunsuits. And ironing. Liza always had a basket of things that needed to be ironed. She didn't really mind doing it; she could listen to the radio, talk to Abby, and think about things. But it was just one of those tasks that seemed to have no end.

She set up the ironing board in their new bright kitchen, and decided to tackle the napkins left from Minx's last visit. Minx had given Liza the napkins when she and Julius were engaged. They had belonged to Minx's mother, and were, as Minx pointed out, "the real thing . . . they simply don't make them like this any more."

Liza stuck the spray nozzle into a Coke bottle filled with water. She sprinkled the napkins. When spread out, each napkin could have almost covered a card table. Soft, creamy damask, with a thick monogram near one corner, the white letters so scrolled and entwined that they were impossible to decipher. Liza had learned from her own mother that the way to make embroidery stand out was to iron it upside down on a thick towel. Liza's mother had been full of esoteric domestic secrets like that: how to wash French doeskin gloves, the best way to clean a polar bear rug, how to store your heirloom lace veil. Secrets you might never need to know.

Liza remembered how she used to hate it when her mother would say, "Remember this for life, Liza," as she imparted some scrap of housekeeping trivia, or some beauty hint, tiny techniques that Liza was already sure she'd never use. Minx, who had never had any reason to concern herself with housewifely activities, and who hired experts to burnish her static image of pseudo-youthfulness, would have laughed herself into a coughing fit over these trifling admonitions.

Steam rose from the napkin, warming Liza's face and moistening her hair. She hummed along with the white plastic radio, ". . . whether I do or don't, whether I will or won't; I'm undecided now." Liza's feet and the iron itself moved to the beat. I'm not undecided, she told herself. Everything has already been decided.

Now Pat Boone crooned from the plastic radio. "Writing love letters . . . in the sand." Liza disliked his syrupy voice, and besides, the music didn't seem to go with what Abby was up to just then. She silenced Pat Boone with a click. Abby was engrossed, not unusually, in playing church. At one end of the kitchen she had lined up little chairs and stools, facing the coffee table, which now held two candlesticks. Abby's doll Rosie sat slumped in the red chair in the middle. Kind Dog, Beary, Whale, and two stuffed rabbits were propped up beside Rosie. Wendell lay with his head on his paws, brown eyes open. In front of each seat Abby had placed one of her Little Golden books.

"Yes, Jesus loves me . . ." Abby, in pink overalls, held an open book in front of her as she sang. Her face was turned from Liza, but the sun lit up her blonde curls. Her halo, Liza thought. Abby's frail soprano floated over the heads of her congregation. ". . . the Bible tells me so."

Oh dear, thought Liza, this all comes from the *one* time we took the poor child to Sunday School. Now Julius says we've got to go every week . . . and ruin Sunday mornings. She thought maybe Abby had A Calling; her mind jumped to the cold stone walls of a convent, far-off ethereal voices in a plainsong, muffled footsteps on the stone floor, rustling habits, Abby's smooth saintly face coiffed in starched white. Then she pictured a dense, far away jungle, ropy vines, snakes dropping from the trees, a greasy green river, straw huts, rows of white cots. "Unclean, unclean," cried the lepers, shaking their little bells. Abby in her voluminous white habit followed close behind the white-bearded doctor, healing with a touch . . .

Stop it, Liza told herself. Now the service was over, and Abby took the church apart. Liza poured her a cup of apple juice, and then went back to ironing.

"Mummy has just a little more to do before lunchtime, sweetie. Can you put everything away like a good girl?"

Am I the bad girl? Liza wondered. The ironed napkins did look nice. She had finished all eight of them before tackling Julius's sanforized shirts and Abby's dresses. Mostly Abby wore corduroy overalls, but Liza liked to put her in a dress for any remotely special occasion. She pulled out a sea green frock, dense with embroidery, that Minx had bought for Abby in Florence. The little puffed sleeves were impossible to iron, one thing Liza's mother never taught her.

They heard the scrunch of tires in the gravel driveway. Wendell lifted his head. Abby went to the big window and pressed her hands to the glass. "Daddy? No . . ." Liza was pressing a pink sash. She waited to see who walked up the path. A tan sportscar, an MG, and then Derek. Her heart seemed to lurch in her chest, a leap of joy. She saw her face reflected in the iron, and pushed at her hair. She looked down at her too-short bluejeans, sagging white socks, her old sneakers with the red laces. She unplugged the iron. Wendell barked.

Abby trailed her to the front door. "Who is it, Mummy?"

"Hi," he said. "I want you to come and see the elephants."

"Elephants? What elephants? I didn't . . . I didn't know you were back from your trip."

"Real elephants. They're at Burbecks' Ice Cream. Come on. I'll bring you home."

"I was just going to fix Abby her lunch."

"Oh, come on. We can have hot dogs there. And ice cream. And elephants."

Liza started to laugh. Abby was saying, "Mummy, Mummy, say yes."

Derek looks so perfectly clean, Liza thought, as they walked down the path. Who irons those khaki pants, that crisp blue shirt so exactly like Julius's but entirely different on this man? He opened the car door and Liza ducked in, holding Abby tightly against herself. It was only a short drive.

"There *are* elephants," Liza said when they pulled into the dusty parking area beside the ice cream stand. "Why are they here?" They climbed out of the car, Liza holding Abby's hand.

There were three elephants, large, medium, and small. The small one was not in fact very small. They were pacing around, one after the other, inside a fenced enclosure no larger than Wendell's yard. The red snow-fencing didn't look nearly substantial enough. The big elephant could step right over it, Liza thought, although it wouldn't even need to. Any one of them could push the fence right over.

The keeper got out of the truck where he'd been sitting. He pushed back his felt hat and squatted beside Abby. "You're a mighty sweet little girl. How about a ride on a big elephant?"

Abby clung to Liza's leg.

"You'll be fine, ma'am — the baby, too," said the keeper. "Only two dollars — fifty cents for the little girl."

The elephants had blue and yellow harnesses. The keeper held a stick with a hook attached to one end. He caught the middle-sized elephant by the harness, and with a few shouts got it to kneel.

"Do you want a ride, Liza?"

"No. No thank you. We're not going to ride," she said firmly.

The keeper shrugged, and climbed back into his pickup truck.

Liza and Derek stood for a while looking at the great gray wrinkled pachyderms, who continued their endless pacing, occasionally snuffling in the dust with their trunks.

"Their eyes are so little, so wise," Liza said.

"Their ears are funny," Abby said, as the elephants shook their soft leathery ears.

"Those yellow tusks — ivory," mused Liza.

"Think of all the piano keys," Derek said.

"I feel they must be very old," Liza said. "even the small one. Maybe hundreds of years old." She kept looking at the elephants, searching for clues.

"I wonder what they think," Derek said. "Do they remember being free?"

"Maybe these elephants were never free," said Liza.

"Oh yes, they were free. Once upon a time they were free, they were happy. Once upon a time, long, long ago."

Liza glanced at Derek. He was looking far away. We're caught, too, she thought. When Derek held out a hand to Liza, she took it. She held Abby in her other arm. They walked across to the ice cream stand.

As soon as Julius came home, Abby rushed to tell him about the elephants.

"Well, that's a funny thing, Abby. I never heard of elephants in Rock Hill. Who did you go with?"

"Derek," Abby said. "He took us, and I had pink ice cream."

Julius straightened up and looked to Liza. "Derek? Hmm. That guy doesn't have enough to do."

LIZA CALLED Billie Ray Ryan to tell her about the elephants. "You should take your boys over. Duane would like it, too. Kids can even have rides." Then she remembered that of course Billie had no car. "I'll take you. We'll all go. Abby would love to see them again." They set a date for Wednesday.

On Monday Billie called. "Oh Liza, we can't go to the elephants. We can't go *anywhere.*"

"Why?" Liza's first thought was, oh-oh, something to do with Tom. She couldn't forget about seeing him necking with that Tilly at their party.

But this was something else. "Dr. Davis says my boys have the *whooping cough.* I have to keep them in quarantine for *six weeks*! Liza, I'm going to go stir crazy, I'm telling you. I truly am."

Liza could hear the boys coughing. "Six weeks!" Her brain was reeling backwards, wondering if and when Abby might have been exposed.

A few days later, Billie called Liza. "My boys are driving me out of my mind, Liza. All I do is bake, bake, bake. Bread, sweet rolls, parker house rolls, hot milk sponge cake, Mama's coconut layer cake, sweet potato pie . . . oh, I just don't know."

And drink Pepsicola, put on more weight, Liza thought. Aloud she said, "I wish there were something I could do."

The next week Billie sounded frantic. "Liza, you won't believe this. My house is full of feathers, and I think I'm losing my mind!"

"Feathers? From a bird? Just tell me, Billie."

Liza heard Billie take a long breath. "Well. I was in the

kitchen," she gulped, ". . . making piccalilli with the last . . . green tomatoes, and my boys were . . .(sniff). . . upstairs, so quiet — and for a few minutes it seemed really peaceful. I was listening to some symphony on the radio . . ." Her voice went up high.

"And then . . .?"

"And then . . . I went out in the hall — and the air was full of *feathers*, all over the floor. Thurman and Donny had found a little bitty hole in my . . . best . . . comforter, and they were up there, ripping, shaking it over the stairs, the two of them, laughing." By now Billie sounded hysterical to Liza, who tried not to laugh herself.

"I didn't know whether to call Tom first, or you. I'm just sitting here, with feathers in my hair, everywhere. Maybe I'll just *leave* it, so Tom can see . . ."

"And my Duane," Billie went on. "She's allergic. The minute she gets off that schoolbus she'll just start right in wheezing — and my boys are still whooping. Oh Liza, what can I do?"

Liza felt her own life to be easy and orderly compared to Billie's. Liza had only one child, which usually made her feel sad and embarrassed, as well as inadequate, but you had to admit it was easier. Also she had a car of her own, so she could go out for groceries, take Abby to Story Hour, things like that. Of course it was true that Julius made more money than Tom; he was at a better law firm. And he had that little trust fund from his father . . .

The whooping cough quarantine finally ended. But Billie was still trapped at home, except on the one day a week when Julius gave Tom a ride to their train so Billie Ray could do her food shopping. Liza started going over to Billie's house quite often, maybe a couple of times a week.

At first she told herself she was just being nice. Abby, of course, loved playing with Thurman and Donny — and she worshipped Duane.

"Boys! Thurman! Donny! Be nice to Abby, you hear?" Billie would caution. "Treat her like a little lady, you hear? She's not used to rough boys."

Liza observed that Billie didn't seem to notice that Abby ran just as fast, and was just as rowdy, as the two boys.

Billie liked to talk, but she listened, too. Before long Liza was telling her things she'd never told anyone before — about her mother, maybe, or about Julius. Sometimes they sat in the living room, but mostly in the cluttered kitchen, redolent with cinnamon. Billie would shoo Mrs. Reed the cat off the rocker, and flick a dish towel across the chair to ready it for Liza. Billie was usually ensconced on a high stool, kneading dough on a slab of marble. She showed Liza how she set bread to rise in the oven of her old gas stove with legs.

"Lay a clean towel over it, like this, and then you leave it over a pan of hot water. The pilot light gives off a little heat, just enough."

Liza's stove was electric and modern, but she thought she should learn to make bread. Billie would get herself another Pepsicola before she'd finished the last one — like chain-smoking, Liza thought — and she'd fix a brown pot of Red Rose tea for Liza. Liza would pour her tea into one of Billie's thick old white ironstone cups, stir honey into it with a thin coin-silver spoon, and sample a slice of Billie's lemon sponge cake, light as feathers. And they'd talk.

"It seems like it's just built in for us to be always mad at our husbands," Billie was saying. "Here they go off every day in their lawyer suits, ride the train, socialize, go out to eat lunch . . ."

"They have no idea how it is for us, " Liza said. "Doing laundry, doing dishes, watching kids, no one to talk to half the time — *most* of the time."

"I've been in Tom's office — cute little secretaries sashaying around on their little spike heels. 'Yes, Mr. Ryan. Right away, Mr. Ryan.' Bringing him coffee. I guess that's what I'm supposed to do when he gets home."

Liza pictured the secretaries as she glanced at Billie's lower legs, firmly planted, clad as always in tan cotton stockings, wide feet running over the edges of her old brown silver-buckled Dr. Scholl's sandals.

"Julius goes to a lunch club once a week. And sometimes he stays late, and plays squash with a friend. He'll call me to keep dinner hot for him. I don't know why, but it always makes me mad when he does that." Liza's cup clattered down so hard she was afraid she'd chipped it.

"There's really no answer, is there? Did you ever used to think it would turn out like this?"

"Oh no," Liza said. "We thought we'd be different, Julius and I — at least, I thought so. More like partners. I used to try to look nice every day. I still do at night, before he gets home. Not that anyone notices."

"I'm lucky if I get to go out once every couple of weeks. Get dressed up for Mr. & Mrs. Club, or a movie. Your party." Liza winced, because that party hadn't turned out well for Billie.

Billie ran her hands down the front of her dark blue dress — she had no lap to speak of. "Can you believe I was Homecoming Queen at Pine Mountain College my sophomore year? I was just a little bit of a thing — red roses — and my white gown . . . " Her eyes were looking far away.

Another day in Billie's kitchen, Liza felt a sudden impulse to talk about Derek. "Billie, have you ever met Ham Clifford's brother?"

Billie and Tom didn't really know the Cliffords all that well, and besides, Tom thought Ham was a right wing snob. Billie had not met Ham's brother.

"His name is Derek. He's not at all like Ham. He plays the piano, and he reads a lot. He graduated from MIT, but he hated it. Now he's supposed to get a Master's degree."

"Is he nice? He sounds pretty young, but then, I always forget how young you are, Liza."

"Yes." Liza thought about it. "He is nice."

"So what are you telling me?"

"Oh, Billie, he's so unhappy. He hates his father, and he hates the idea of working at the granite quarry. But he doesn't know what else to do." Liza shook her head slowly. "He's pretty lonely, actually, and he can't see any way out."

"He sounds like us, Liza. Or me anyhow."

"Maybe, in a way. I really . . . well, I like him. But . . ."

"Liza, honey, does he like you?"

"I guess so. But it's not really like that . . . We just sort of . . . talk about things." Liza looked up at the flaking plaster ceiling, at the row of old tan crocks on the top shelf.

"Does Julius know?"

"Oh! He knows Derek — a little — but I'd absolutely die if he *ever* found out how much I . . ."

Billie stood up, walked over and put her arms around Liza, a thing she'd never done before. Billie smelled as sweet as her own fresh bread.

"Don't you worry, Liza. You're so good, you'd never let things go too far. So keep dreaming; sometimes that's all we have."

Liza didn't think Billie understood that this was more than dreams. She knew she wasn't as good a person as Billie thought she was. But still, Liza felt better, having told.

Billie made her have another cup of Red Rose tea and a slice of new bread. "Try some of my peach preserves — I did them a different way. Sometime I'll tell you about the carpenter we had here last summer, working on the new roof. Oh, land, nothing happened, but . . . he was so handsome." Billie's smooth lovely face had a dreamy expression. "And he did like my chess pie. . . ." They heard the children rushing down the stairs.

Story Hour

LIZA STARTED taking Abby to the Tuesday morning Story Hour at the library. She and Abby would tromp up the bare wooden stairs to the second floor room where the stuffed birds were. With her black lace-up orthopedic shoes planted squarely in front of her, Miss Oletha Day sat in the one full-size chair, presiding over a circle of ten tiny chairs. Other children drifted in, followed by the mothers. Abby cared more about the children than the stories, most of which she'd heard at home anyway.

While things were getting under way, Liza circled the room, looking at the dusty larks and sparrows behind glass doors. Their bald spots made her sad. The bluebird was no longer what you'd call blue. The red-tailed hawk's head had flopped to one side, making him look more like a victim than a majestic bird of prey. One cabinet held a mysterious collection: two gold-and-purple painted plates, a silver punch ladle, a pointed stone, corroded coins, some frayed military decorations, and, framed in gilt and velvet, three unidentified daguerrotypes, so black you could scarcely see the staring century-old faces. On the mauve-red walls above hung Abraham Lincoln and a few noted Rock Hill-ians, eyeing her malevolently. Miss Oletha Day began to read. "Once upon a time . . . " The most magical words in all the world, thought Liza, as she turned to leave.

She walked downstairs with Peg Reilly and Gladys Shoemaker. "How about coming over for coffee?" Gladys said. "I just fried up a batch of doughnuts; Skipper loves them, ha ha."

Recalling Skipper Shoemaker's chins and the way his plaid shirts bowed out over his belt, Liza thought he ate too many of Gladys's doughnuts. The Shoemakers' house was just across the Common from the library. Liza remembered the matched set of copper-bottomed saucepans hanging on Gladys's kitchen wall, gleaming pink like new, and causing guilt pangs in Liza at the thought of her own pans, wedding presents, their copper coating now streaky and brown. You were supposed to polish them every single day.

"That's very nice of you," Liza said. "But I think I'll take a walk; I need some exercise. Want to come?"

At the bottom of the granite steps, by the stone lions, they turned in opposite directions. Liza was sure they thought her odd as well as rude. Peg and Gladys were always so busy, if you listened to them. Canning and freezing. Knitting sweaters for all their kids. Making jelly. Baking all their own bread. They probably couldn't imagine just going for a plain walk.

She was going round the corner of the yellow brick building when she saw Derek come out, a green book bag over his shoulder. She took a deep breath.

"Liza," he said. "I've never seen you here before."

She waited while he caught up with her. "Abby's at the Story Hour. Every Tuesday. Last week was her first, and she loved it." She felt as if she were trying to justify her presence there.

"So the mothers have a little time off."

"I just said no to coffee at Gladys Shoemaker's 'cause I wanted some fresh air."

Liza could see Gladys and Peg walking into Gladys's house. Of course they'll see me talking to Derek, she realized. Peg never misses anything. They'll probably think I *planned* to meet him. Well, I didn't! "I've always wanted to walk out here," she said. "Such a beautiful view."

Derek walked with her. They kicked through red and yellow maple leaves, heading behind the library toward a gap in a stone wall, where tall pines framed faraway hills and cerulean sky.

"The tall one is Mount Monadnock," Derek told her. "From the top of Monadnock you can see the Rock Hill church spire. And from here you can see the gold dome of the State House, if it's clear."

It seemed to Liza that he was sharing a secret with her. But sighting the gold dome with Julius would not be the same. She felt confused.

Derek lifted the bar of a farm gate, and they walked across a sloping rocky pasture, where a few Holstein heifers looked up briefly from their grazing. Following a cart track, thick with fallen yellow needles, Liza and Derek walked through pine woods.

"You've probably been here a million times," Liza said.

"Father used to bring Ham and me out here, after he got us our first shotguns. I was about eight. He'd get so mad when I missed a bird."

"You were *eight*?"

"One time I cried." Derek's face was impassive. "He hit me over the head with the stock of his gun."

Liza winced. "And you were just a little boy!" She turned to Derek. He was looking straight ahead; his face didn't change. The pine needles were soft beneath their feet. They walked on without speaking.

They both spotted the bird's nest, lying where it had fallen beside the trail. Derek picked it up. The hollow inside was smooth and silky soft with bits of moss and down. With two fingers Liza stroked it.

"Think of the work that went into this," she murmured.

"A safe place for the babies — as safe as they could make it, those birds."

"Everyone needs a safe place."

Liza gasped when she heard the church bell strike noon. "Derek, I have to get back."

"Cinderella. Well." He shrugged, and she walked quickly on ahead.

When she got to the gate, she turned to look back. Derek stood where she'd left him. He didn't wave when she held up her hand, but she knew he saw her.

Almost every Tuesday after that Liza ran into Derek at the library. Once they met in the fiction stacks by the H's, where Liza had pulled out *The Sun also Rises.*

"Oh." She was startled when his shadow suddenly blocked the light at the end of the aisle. "I didn't hear you."

Derek reached out for the book she was holding. "Good choice." He smiled at her.

When she reached to take it back from him, she felt the warmth of his hand.

Liza's heart was pounding as she left him and climbed down the steep metal stairs from the stacks. Probably just her fear of heights. At the desk she handed the book to Miss Bynum, the librarian.

"Your card?"

"Oh! I'm sorry." Liza fumbled around in her bag, hoping that Miss Bynum wouldn't notice her flushed face. Miss Bynum stamped in the date, and, looking right at Liza, said, "Fine weather we're getting. How's Mister?"

One cold day, just before Thanksgiving, Liza walked again with Derek into the woods. The pine needles were silvered with frost. She was wearing her white bunny fur earmuffs. Derek had a red scarf around his neck.

They didn't talk much. They never did. Derek bent over and picked up a stone, small, round, and pure white. He rolled it in his palm, then held it out to Liza. She looked at him and dropped the stone into the pocket of her camel's hair coat.

When he stopped suddenly, and said, "What are you so afraid of, Liza?" she saw his breath come out in puffy clouds, warm from inside him. Their eyes met. When he put his arms around her, she felt herself clinging, yearning. His breath warmed her, his scarf was scratchy on her cheek. Her earmuffs fell onto the frosty ground.

A Serious Talk

THE PHONE rang as Liza was just finishing up the dinner dishes.

"I'll get it," she called. Julius was at his desk in the other room, paying bills.

"Liza. This is Derek."

"Oh, hi." Her voice got thin, the way it sometimes did when she heard Derek's voice.

He had never telephoned before. She looked at the narrow gold watch that had been her mother's, as if the time had a special significance. Ten past eight.

"I'd like to talk to Julius."

Her thumping heart seemed to stop. She couldn't think of anything to say, and she couldn't say it anyway. But why, why, why? she asked herself as she put down the receiver. She stood there for a moment, looking at the black phone as if it were alive, then walked to the door of Julius's study.

"It's Derek Clifford," she said, still in that thin tight voice, hoping Julius wouldn't notice. "He would like to talk to you." Julius frowned when he looked at her on his way to the telephone.

Liza set out their two blue coffee cups for the morning. She wiped off the counters, wiping until she realized she had done the same counter at least twice.

"Wednesday night's OK," she heard Julius saying. "Around eight? Sure. See you then."

Would Julius tell her anything? Would he think it strange if she didn't even ask? Still swabbing away, she tried to make her voice sound ordinary. She asked, not looking at Julius, "What's up with Derek?"

Julius was heading back to his desk. "Oh, he's coming over to ask my advice."

Liza put the sponge down. She was startled. "Advice?" Gazing at the half-moon dents her fingernails had made in the palm of her hand, she thought, maybe this has nothing to do with me.

"About his future. He needs my help. You know, to decide what to do. With his life."

Liza heard the note of pride in Julius's voice. He shrugged as if it weren't important, but Liza saw his tight pleased smile. She watched him sit down again at his desk, just sitting there, twirling his silver letter opener. He's in awe of those Cliffords, she decided. All of them. Even Derek.

Liza didn't want to see Derek when he came over to talk to Julius. She just couldn't. Well before Derek was due to arrive she headed upstairs with laundry to fold, plus Hemingway to read. She even got undressed, put on her flannel wrapper and slippers. She froze when she heard Derek come into their house.

"Would you like a beer?" she heard Julius say. The answer must have been no, for almost immediately came the sound of the study door being firmly shut. Against me, she thought.

It seemed an eternity before she heard the door open again. "Well, best of luck," Julius said. "I'm sure it will work out."

Derek's voice was only a soft buzz, then his sportscar was loud in the driveway. Liza watched his headlights turn down the road until they disappeared.

Liza was reading in bed when Julius's feet came clomping up the stairs. She had vowed to say nothing, ask nothing. As if she didn't care a bit. Let Julius tell her if he wanted to. Long after he was snoring gently, Liza lay there thinking, watching the beam of light that washed across the room every time a car went by.

Not until the next morning did Julius refer to Derek's visit. "He's really got problems, Derek has. Doesn't know what to do."

"Oh?" Liza was slicing a banana for Abby. She didn't look up.

"He wants to go to graduate school; his dad wants him to start right in at the quarry; he's not sure he wants any part of it. Then he talks about music!"

"So what did you tell him?"

"I said he should do both. Persuade his father that a Master's degree would be good for Clifford Granite. And it would."

"But he *hates* his father!" The words exploded. She put her thumb to her mouth and bit down hard.

"Liza! What do you know? He asked me, and I told him."

Why, oh why, had Derek ever thought Julius could help him?

"Is my toast ready yet? Bring the jam, too. You know most people would give anything to have a good job just waiting for them, a family business. Derek doesn't seem to have any idea how lucky he is."

Liza tried to act neutral, uninterested. She took a deep breath. "Mmm." She watched Abby carefully scooping up a banana slice with her spoon, and looked out at Wendell, snuffling for rabbits under the big hemlock. She saw the bright morning sun light up the last red leaves on the top of the big oak.

Julius crunched on his toast. "Actually, to tell the truth, I don't think too much of him. Now Ham — and Mr. Clifford — I don't agree with them on a lot of things, politics and all, but you have to hand it to them. They're strong. Ham really takes after their father. But Derek — well, Derek's weak."

Liza spent most of the morning doing laundry. What would Julius say, she wondered, if I were to tell him I wanted a divorce? She folded Julius's pajamas, his underwear. She matched up his socks, rolling them into tight black balls. Would I want a divorce? No, she told herself finally. I belong here. One sock had a hole in the toe. She set it aside.

Third Man II

"WHOA. ANOTHER party at Le Pigeonnier." Julius rolled his eyes when Liza told him. But of course they would go. He never said this, but Liza knew that the Cliffords' parties reminded Julius of all the parties he'd gone to in college, and all the parties he'd missed while he was grinding his way through law school; Saturday nights in the library. Liza could almost read his thoughts now in his tight smile and the far-away look in his eyes. Those remembered parties, half imagined, crowded with beautiful people, laughing, drinking, never at a loss for the perfect repartee.

"You'd better line up Peggy Sue's mother to stay over," Julius told Liza. "It'll be late, you know."

Liza was the one who was uneasy about this party. She felt clenched, imagining how it would be. I'll stay far away from Derek, she told herself; just act neutral, talk to other people.

Late Monday evening, before the weekend of the Cliffords' Christmas party, the phone rang. It was almost eleven. Julius was already asleep, and Liza was about to turn the light out.

"Hello Liza, sweetie." A familiar male voice.

"Bunny!" Liza exclaimed, smiling already. Across the bed she saw Julius's eyes pop open, and a scowl furrow his brow. Bunny Hopkins was so amusing, so bizarre, actually, such a refreshing contrast to all the other aspects of her current life.

"Yeah, this is your bad old friend from the big bad city. Actually, dearie, I've just got to get the hell out of Manhattan. Can you rescue me this weekend? Will you be around?"

"Well — sure. Do come."

"Oh sweetie, you're such a dear. I really need a dose of that brisk New England air."

Liza wasn't sure she liked that. And she couldn't forget how he'd complained about the lack of heat on his last visit.

"I'll try to catch the one o'clock on Friday. Tell Julius I'll walk to his office from South Station, around five-ish. How is old Jules, anyhow?"

Julius's eyes were closed now; Liza still saw his frown. But Bunny was his friend! "You know we both love to have you. Any time. And a couple of things are going on you might like." She could picture him at the Cliffords'. He might make everything easier.

On Saturday night the Cliffords' circular driveway was filled with cars — mostly Jaguars and MGs, it looked like — when Julius, Liza, and Bunny drove up in the Henry J. They parked down the street, and walked through softly falling snow. The cars were already veiled in white. Liza tipped her head back, opening her mouth to catch the downy flakes on her tongue.

Bunny had known Ham Clifford at college. Now he was recalling the one time he had been to Le Pigeonnier.

"That was a night to remember. 1953, June, it would have been. Will we see Paulette tonight? It was her party. She was a wild little thing!"

"She got married and moved out West somewhere, that's all I know," Liza said.

"Lake Forest." As usual, Julius knew.

"Wonder if she married the guy that got her tossed out of Pine Manor! *Big* scandal." Bunny giggled. "The party was something else, a tent over the whole garden. Lester Lanin himself, playing. Dom Perignon pouring like water. Scrambled eggs when the sun came up — you know, the whole works. Nothing but the best for Paulette. Daddy's little darlin'."

When they came in, the big room was packed with people. Over their heads the air was blue with cigarette smoke and the sweet smell of Christmas greens. Bunny and Ham slapped each other on the back in a semblance of a hug. Liza heard the pounding of the piano. Only the bass notes came through the din. I'm not going to the piano, she told herself. Looking at the other wives, Liza felt underdressed. Her old black velvet, cut low in front, seemed too plain, too short, too narrow. She found Evvy. They could barely hear each other. Julius brought Liza a glass of amber-colored punch and a red napkin. Then he disappeared.

"What's in it?" But Evvy, who was drinking it too, couldn't hear.

"Are Mr. and Mrs. Clifford here?" Liza shouted in Evvy's ear.

"Ma Cliff's around, but Ham's dad is off some place like Pennsylvania. Boar hunting with Uncle Shep. He wanted Ham to go. They do it every year."

"Boar hunting! You mean wild boar?"

"Aah, who knows. Any boar would go wild when it saw those guys aiming their rifles."

It was too hard to talk. Liza turned away, trying not to see Derek. Shrill women's voices rose above the noise.

"You've gotta see our new bathroom. All red. Red toilet! Don't you love it?" A cackle of laughter.

"Buddy's only three, but you bet your booties he skis. He doesn't want to be left behind!"

"Oh, we've got a ton of canned food in there, but I keep telling Shep if we had to spend a week in our shelter with five kids —"

The stern-faced men, in tight little clusters, talked to each other. "The State Department is *still* riddled with Communists. This guy I know, a lawyer down in DC, he told me . . ."

Liza looked around for Bunny. He was standing, talking, gesticulating, by a sofa, where beautiful Valerie, the

Cliffords' cousin, sat with Miguel, the granite expert from Portugal. Why is he here *again*? He's married, Mrs. Clifford had told Liza. With four babies back home. Liza couldn't forget that. He and Valerie lay back, laughing up at Bunny. Valerie, in a smooth creamy long dress that clung to her, and no glitter except for dangly green earrings, outshone all the wives in their red dresses, their ruffles, their spangles, thought Liza. Next to Bunny was another man, dark and foreign-looking in a wide-shouldered checked jacket nipped tight at his waist.

Liza edged over to Bunny, who put an arm around her and kept on talking.

"So the elevator door opens, and, I kid you not, it's the *same* little blue-haired lady, swathed in sable, dripping with diamonds, and clutching this *revolting* little dog. 'Oh, it's yew,' she says . . ." Bunny pursed his lips, and spoke in a falsetto. His listeners laughed, and Liza laughed too, even though she didn't know what he was talking about.

"Liza, this is Paolo, Miguel's brother," Valerie said. Liza held out her hand. Paolo bowed low to kiss it. Valerie's voice was so low that they all leaned close to hear what she was saying.

"Paolo's only here for ten days. We're trying to persuade him to come to Franconia with us. At New Year's."

"No, no, no." Paolo's accent was strong. "You are so kind, but unfortunately I must be in New York City at that time."

Liza saw Bunny's eyes fasten on Paolo for an instant, fall away, and then return to meet Paolo's dark-eyed gaze. The look on Bunny's face was vaguely familiar. She was reminded of something — a dream, probably. But Bunny, always so self-assured, seemed suddenly vulnerable. He still had an arm hung loosely over her shoulder. Liza leaned closer for a moment before she pulled away. Derek, she noticed, was no longer at the piano.

Mrs. Clifford, whom Liza had not seen before, came into the room clapping her hands. She called out into the noise, "Food! Food, children, in the dining room." Liza thought no one could hear her, but slowly people trickled in to fill fancy old blue and gilt plates with ham and macaroni and Waldorf salad in the rosy aura of red candles.

Liza carried her plate and another glass of punch back to the big room. There was nowhere to sit. People were crowded onto all the sofas; others sat shoulder to shoulder on the steps. No one was sitting on the piano bench, so Liza wound across the room. Empty punch glasses flanked the keyboard. She willed Derek to come back. She was waiting for something to happen. She and he hadn't even spoken to each other yet. Sipping her punch, Liza wondered idly what was in it. It might be very strong, she thought, underneath the fruitiness. She had a fuzzy feeling in her head, as if nothing mattered.

Then Derek was sitting beside her, not speaking, not even looking at her. He was playing *The Third Man* theme, the tune that had seemed so haunting when she'd first heard him play it, at another Clifford party, more than a year ago. Now it sounded bleak and lonely. Liza was perched on one end of the bench, but Derek seemed miles away. What was wrong? He was bent over the keys. When he wasn't smiling, his cheeks were hollow.

Without planning it, she cupped her hands around his neat pale ear. "Derek," she breathed. She felt as if she were someone else. Her lips touched his ear. He stopped playing, turned to look at her. Surprising herself, Liza laughed. Derek smiled, and Liza's world was fine.

"What's so funny?" he asked her.

"You know those Tabu ads? Tabu perfume? They were always in *Life* magazine; you probably didn't even notice. But when I was fifteen, my friend Amy and I used to go wild over that picture. We wanted it to be us!"

"What *are* you talking about?" Derek, still smiling, was shaking his head.

"Oh, it was so shocking. The lady in the hoop skirt was playing the piano, and the man, this dashing, handsome violinist with sideburns, just *flung* away his bow, and grabbed her." Liza lowered her brow, and fixed Derek with a mock sinister glare. "Ta*boo*," she purred, lingering over the last syllable.

"What made you think of that?"

"Oh, there's no connection." Liza felt as if she were floating. I love him.

"Do you want to try it?"

"Well . . ." She tilted her head. Then, "No!" She drew back. She stood up, knocking over her empty glass.

"No, Derek." She held up a warning finger. "People would notice. After all, I have to think of my reputation." She rolled her eyes.

Derek shrugged. His hands began moving on the keys again. Liza turned away. What do I want? she asked herself.

She wondered suddenly where Julius was. She felt as if the sight of him would make everything normal again. She couldn't see him. Some people had already left the party. She saw Valerie and Miguel, side by side on their sofa. A woman called Angie something lay on the rug with her glittery dress hiked up around her knees, shoes off, her feet in Pete Poole's lap.

Liza looked in at the door of Mr. Clifford's book-lined library. Julius was there. A lamp shaded in green glass lit up a green felt table top in one corner of the dark room. Neat stacks of red and white chips, overflowing ashtrays, and half-filled glasses made a frieze around the table.

"I'll see you, and I'll raise you," Julius was saying to Ham, as he put down two chips. A man called Chet was playing, plus two men whose names Liza didn't know, and Portia, the only woman. Each of them held a fan of shining cards.

The crowd had definitely thinned out. Liza looked around for Evvy. She finally found her in the kitchen, squinched up in the breakfast nook, talking earnestly with Shep. Deciding not to interrupt, Liza turned away.

Bunny seemed to have vanished, too. Julius and I should have kept an eye on him, she thought, with a pang. After all, he didn't know a soul, except for Ham. She peered out a window, the glass cool against her forehead. Downy snowflakes were dropping fast through the triangle of light from an upper window. She heard a car revving up, and moving slowly out toward the road.

She went into the big room again. She knew the song Derek was playing. "By the deep . . ." she hummed, "and pearly waters . . . white silver sands." For a minute she thought that no one else was in the room, but Valerie and Miguel were still there, and a few others. A man with his jacket off lay asleep or passed out on one of the leather sofas. His gray pants were wrenched up over the tops of red and green argyle socks — probably knit by his wife, Liza thought — exposing a strip of white leg. One loafer dangled from his toes; the other sat forlornly on the oriental rug, next to an empty glass. The piano drowned whatever noises might be coming from that fallen open mouth.

Liza stood in the doorway, listening, looking. Then she was walking across the room, walking toward Derek as if she were being pulled. Leaning on the piano, she looked down at his long fingers, his blunt pale nails, moving on the keys. Like dancing, it was. Now his hands would stretch wide, a thumb arced back to strike one note, while the little finger reached, reached the other way. Then his fingers would move quickly, like darting minnows, rippling, tickling. The next minute his hands were hammers, beating, pounding so you thought the keys must cry out in pain. Liza felt the pounding, and closed her eyes.

"Somewhere I'll find you. Moonlight behind you . . ." Derek was singing an old Noel Coward song that Liza had always loved. His brown hair ended in soft golden down at the back of his head. With one finger Liza touched his neck. She felt like resting her cheek there, so cool.

He stopped playing, and stood up. With his hand on her elbow, he walked her to a now-empty sofa by the fireplace. Liza sat on the edge.

"I have to know something." She was serious. "Remember the night you came over to talk to Julius?"

"Of course I remember. I was wondering where you were."

"I was there, upstairs. But, well, I was surprised. What made you think Julius could help you?"

"Listen, he married *you*. It seemed as though he had everything under control. Unlike most people I know."

"Well, did he? Help, I mean."

"He said it was up to me, but if he were in my shoes he'd stick with the family business."

"So. Is that what you're going to do?"

"Very likely. I don't know. But . . . maybe I won't." He laughed, but it was short and hard. Liza flinched.

A log sank onto the coals, sending up a crackling shower of sparks. Liza saw the glow reflected on Derek's face.

He turned to her. "You look beautiful in the light."

Liza felt suddenly weak with desire. "Oh . . ."

Derek stood up and took her two hands in his, lifting her. Liza leaned her head against his shoulder. With his arm around her, they walked out into the hall. Lit only by the light from the gun cabinet, the hall was dark and empty. They stood at the foot of the red-carpeted stairs. The walls were red, glowing warm. The air smelled of candles and the sweet needled evergreens. The space under the stairs made a secret cave, the warm red walls deepened to crimson. Liza heard herself moan as they leaned into each other, pressing close. Derek smelled like evergreens. She felt his fingers ripple down her spine as though he were playing scales. Standing there swaying, they nuzzled, they murmured, they kissed.

Suddenly they were hit by a fall of yellow light from a door opening down the hall. Liza pulled away from Derek, stunned, blinded. Voices followed the light, voices and hoots of laughter. The woman called Portia came out of the open door, tottering on high heels. "I'm never gonna play poker with you guys again," she was saying, not meaning it.

Liza heard Ham's voice, and then Julius's, rising, falling, boasting, joking. Flustered and confused, Liza pushed at her hair and smoothed her dress. In almost the same instant she heard feet starting down the stairs. She couldn't think whether to move or stay. Derek stood by the stair rail, his arms at his sides, his face closed.

Then Bunny appeared, bounding down the stairs, hair flying, his red ascot dangling from one hand. "Were you looking for me?" Bunny's eyes darted from Liza to Derek and back to Liza. "It's late! Time to go home. Is Jules champing at the bit?"

Now Portia was among them, and the other poker players, all talking and arguing amicably. Bunny became part of the merry crowd.

"Come on, Liza," said Julius when he noticed her. "And Bunny, old man. Time to hit the road." Julius clapped a hand on Liza's shoulder as if he owned her.

"I have to get my coat," she said. She shot another look at Derek, still standing there, the one silent person on the fringe of the gabbling group.

Slowly Liza climbed the stairs. She could feel her heart beating in the empty hollow of her chest. It's over, she told herself. It's hopeless. That's all there is. When she came down again, in her fur-topped boots, her furry earmuffs, and her old camel's hair coat, Derek had vanished.

Bunny seemed her ally now. "I'm glad you're here," she told him as they followed Julius out into the snow.

"I'm glad, too." Bunny patted her on the head as if she were a child. Liza smiled.

BUNNY HAD to head back to New York the day after the Cliffords' party, although he had planned to stay over until Monday. Liza had seen him huddled over the phone that Sunday morning, still in his paisley silk robe and backless brown slippers. Then he'd shuffled out to the kitchen, unshaven, his hair rumpled. Julius was hidden behind the financial pages of the *Globe*. Liza was cutting toast into tiny squares for Abby.

"Sorry, dearies, but things have come up," Bunny said. "You know how it is. Absolutely devastating, rushing away like this."

Bunny took a cup of coffee with him while he ambled off to dress and pack. At the door, he turned and winked at Liza. She felt her face flushing pink. Why is he winking at me, she wondered. As if we had some secret together.

"Mommy, mommy, my toast needs jam. Dolly wants jam, too."

Later Liza and Abby stood by the door, waving to Bunny. Julius was driving him to catch the train for New York.

The week before the Cliffords' party, Julius had suggested to Liza that they invite Ham and Evvy over for a family evening before Christmas.

"Shall we ask the Ryans too?" Liza asked. "Billie Ray tends to get homesick around the holidays."

"No, no. Keep it simple." Julius liked to argue law and politics with Tom, but Liza knew that, for him, the Ryans and the Cliffords were like milk and pickles: they just didn't go. Liza, on the other hand, thought they should bring their two best sets of friends together. Oh well.

Liza called Evvy. "We really want to see you guys, just us, so we can talk. No, not a party. Come early and bring E. It'll be our last chance before Julius's mother comes. Minx. She's spending Christmas here, *three* nights!"

Liza was busy all that week, cleaning Minx's room, making casseroles ahead, and wrapping presents. She kept thinking about Derek, reliving their words, their kiss. It'll probably never happen again, she told herself. She imagined other scenarios, how he scooped her up like the Tabu violin man, how they found an old empty maid's room out behind the kitchen, how he gazed into her eyes and kissed them shut as he tenderly slid the zipper down the back of her velvet dress . . .

Billie called up. "I'm so tired," she said, breathing into the phone. "I've been baking all day, four fruitcakes and three kinds of cookies."

"I haven't done any cookies yet." Liza had a sinking feeling. "I've gotta do that tomorrow."

"It takes my mind off things, keeping busy that way. And my boys just love decorating the gingerbread men."

Naturally, Liza couldn't tell her about the Cliffords' party, since the Ryans hadn't been invited, even though that was the main thing on her mind. She half wished she could tell Billie all about Derek.

The next day Liza made gingerbread men with Abby. The dough stuck to the board, and Liza got cross, but Abby happily stuck in the raisin eyes and buttons. The best cookie looked like Winston Churchill in one of his air raid suits.

On Thursday, Liza and Abby set up the crèche and trimmed the tree. "No, no, honey, the camel can't sleep there; he's too big to go in the manger." Then, "No Abby, sweetie, that's not candy, it's an angel." By then the angel was minus its halo. "Wendell! Bad dog." He'd consumed four candy canes and broken a few more before a tearful Abby caught him in the act. Liza handed Abby the unbreakable tree ornaments, and Abby hung them in a clump on one low branch. Liza was up on a chair ladder trying to fasten the silvery star to the tree when she realized that while she kept busy it could seem as though everything had gone almost back to normal.

ON FRIDAY evening, Julius was just home when the Cliffords arrived. E, who was not yet two, made a grand entrance, wearing red knitted pants, a red sweater, and a red cap with a white tassle on top. Attached somehow to his soft little chin was a beard of fluffy white cotton. Abby laughed. "Baby Santa Claus," she crowed.

"Oh Julius, your camera," Liza said. Julius got a few shots with the flash before E's beard fell off.

Julius made the drinks, and they all sat around the fire. "We should sing," Evvy said, so they did. First "Away in a Manger" and "Jingle Bells," Abby's choices. Liza passed potato chips and a dip.

"Mmm," said Ham, pitching in.

"Oh it's just that dried onion soup thing," Liza said, glancing at Evvy. "I told you I wasn't going to fuss."

"Yum. What did you say it was?" Ham asked, helping himself. "Great flavor."

Then they sang "Joy to the World," and Ham startled them with his booming bass. "And wonders of his love . . ." he growled.

"Well, he was in the Glee Club at college," Evvy said.

Julius stared at Ham, his eyes wide. "I didn't know you could sing."

Later, they put E down in his folding crib, and Liza tucked Abby in upstairs. Julius and Ham and Evvy drank more bourbon and water in the kitchen, while Liza warmed garlic bread and tossed the salad.

"That was quite a party the other night," Julius said. "I missed seeing your father, Ham. He was away?"

"Yeah, boar hunting, and a turkey raffle. Happens every year. I was supposed to be there, as a matter of fact. Dad won it, actually."

"Won the turkey?" Liza wanted to know.

"Um-hmm. And the shoot." Ham made it sound like nothing.

"Anything I can do?" Evvy asked.

Liza had her light the candles on their new Danish teak kitchen table, which just seated four.

"Mmm, what's this?" Ham sniffed, as he dug into the casserole.

"American chop suey," Liza told him.

"Ah so. Me chinka-chinka China man."

Liza looked at Ham. Could he really be Derek's brother? With his forefingers he was pulling the corners of his eyes outward, and tucking his lower lip under his front teeth.

"Well, not actually Chinese," she said. "It's just called that. Hamburger, macaroni, tomatoes from a can."

"Ham, you've had it before," Evvy said. "At Pete and Portia's. And I'd make it, too, if I knew how."

"Did you know Derek came to talk to me?" Julius looked at Ham. "About his future."

"Derek's acting like a spoiled brat," Ham said. "He should come to work at the E. H. Clifford Company *tomorrow*, instead of all this whining and complaining."

"Probably he'll be drafted as soon as he gets out of MIT," Evvy said. "That would take care of him for a while."

Liza felt a pounding in her head. She stood up quickly, and carried plates to the sink. The draft! She'd never thought of it applying to anyone she knew. Ham's voice sounded far away: "Best thing that could happen."

And then, amazingly, they were onto another topic. Derek was still on her mind so much that she couldn't believe it didn't show. Even sharp-eyed Evvy, her friend, had never once commented on the times Liza had walked and talked with Derek, or sat next to him at the piano. But then — Liza shivered — maybe Evvy *had* noticed, and just thought it was perfectly ordinary, married, grown-up behavior, not worth mentioning.

Everybody was finished, so Liza served dessert and Evvy cleared. She'd made one of those chocolate icebox cakes with cookies and whipped cream; if you cut it at an angle it came out in perfect stripes.

"Wow-ee," said Ham. "She's quite the cook, eh Jules?" Then he went on. "So how long did your faggot friend stay? Bunny . . ." Ham affected a drawl, and held out a drooping wrist.

Julius sat up straight. "Bunny? What do you mean? He's your friend, too."

"Oh I *knew* him. In college. But he's not exactly the type I'd want to keep up with."

Liza could tell that this was a revelation to Julius, something that had never occurred to him. Looking at his stricken face, she felt like putting her arm around him, but even had they been alone Julius would shake her off.

No one had much to say after that; the evening dimmed down like a flashlight when the battery starts to go. "Save a weekend after New Year's," Evvy said. "We want you to come skiing at Mittersill. Ham's dad belongs." Soon she was saying, "Ham, it's late. We've gotta go."

Ham carried E, a small beardless sleeping red Santa, while Liza tried to tuck his grayish yellow blanket around him.

"Hope you survive Christmas," Evvy called as they went out.

"Same to you."

"ONE. TWO. Three. *Four*." Abby was counting her grand-mother's bags as Julius carried them into the house.

"Five, Abby dear," Minx held out her arm, a Bonwit Teller shopping bag suspended from it. "Oh, and my purse makes six."

Too much luggage for three days, Liza thought. But then, Minx was not used to traveling light, and besides, it was Christmas. Today she was all in black, unusual for Minx, who usually wore vivid colors. Her high-collared coat, snug at the waist, fanned out so long and so wide that when she turned it lashed Abby in the face and knocked a china ashtray off the hall table.

"Sorry, dearie," Minx said. "So clumsy."

Even though it was not yet noon, she did seem a bit tottery on her pencil legs and high-heeled shoes. The black felt hat perched on the side of her head was wreathed with a veil that dotted her white face with black. Greeting Liza, she held out black-gloved hands. They leaned together and Liza drank in the familiar fragrance of Minx's L'Heure Bleue. As they kissed the air near each other's cheek, the long feather in Minx's hat brushed unpleasantly against Liza's eye. The visit had barely begun, and already Liza was torn by admiration and envy, insecurity and fury. With Minx she always felt like a backward child.

"You must be exhausted, dearie. Little cheeks so hollow." Minx tapped Liza's face with a black-red varnished fingertip. "The house looks adorable — a sweet little tree. And Abby, my pet, such a big girl — much too big for that old thumb!"

Abby stood with her thumb in her mouth, where it often went when she felt bewildered or overwhelmed. Just then Julius opened the door to the kitchen, releasing Wendell, who bounded in, yapping. He jumped up on Minx, almost tipping her over.

"Down, boy, down. A little training needed, I see."

"Sorry, Ma. We *are* taking him to dog school." Poor Julius, Liza thought, Minx puts him on the defensive, too.

Julius had put all his mother's bags in her room. The square red cosmetic bag that accompanied her everywhere, filled with jars and bottles, stood open on the bureau. Minx's voice came from the closet: "Would you be a dear, Liza, and bring me some more hangers? I always find these wire ones impossible, don't you?"

That night, the night before Christmas Eve, Minx curled up after dinner in a corner of the sofa in front of the fire that Julius was busily tending. Again Minx was in black, a narrow swath of velvet to her ankles. If she were in mourning, Liza couldn't imagine for whom; black must be chic this year. Heavy gold bracelets rattled on her bony wrists as she reached for the whiskey and soda that Julius brought her. She was telling Liza and Julius about some couple they didn't know.

"They're just your age. She's such a darling; Liza, you'd adore Tessa. Jules, you must remember Christopher. You and he used to play together when we lived in Oyster Bay. He's something high up in the bank now. I saw a lot of them at Hobe Sound last year when they were visiting Tessa's mother. Now we see each other all the time."

"Ma, I don't know these people." And I don't want to, was what Liza knew Julius was thinking.

"They have a *charming* house — Tessa's done wonders. *Five* children, though you'd never guess it, looking at her. And the most wonderful old-fashioned nanny, so Tessa's able to get out for tennis, lunch parties . . ."

I hate them, Liza was thinking.

"Why are you telling us about these people?" Julius had

raised his voice. "We don't live like that, and we don't want to, do we, Liza?"

Liza loved brave Julius right then. They were a team. But, still, she felt a tiny pang, picturing that Tessa and her perfect life.

"But you could, you know. I just can't bear having you live like hermits in this Godforsaken place, and both working much too hard. You never get out, do you, my poor Liza." Minx reached over to pat Liza's hand. She held out her glass to Julius. "Would you be a dear and bring me a tiny refill?"

Oh dear, thought Liza. Another drink? Minx had had her usual martinis, then red wine with dinner, and now . . . Julius came back with her drink in one hand, and his glass of milk in the other.

"I'm going to turn in, leave you gals to chat. G'night, Ma. Be sure to turn the heat down, Liza."

Alone with Minx, late at night. Liza's brain flashed back for a second to the first time she set foot on the Tilt-a-Whirl at the Dole County Fair, knowing she was in for a bumpy ride.

Minx fanned her hands out in front of her. She seemed to be checking on her red nails. Liza noticed that her lips were the exact same shade as her fingertips.

"How are you, darling? Really, I mean." Tilting her head, Minx fixed Liza's eyes with her own.

Liza pulled herself back, just an inch or two. "Oh I'm fine, thank you." Just as though this were an ordinary conversation.

"But now Julius — I adore him, of course, but really, he's so stuffy. How *is* your life? Do you have *any* life together? Oh you know what I mean, dearie; in bed and all."

"Yes, fine . . . thanks."

Liza wanted to get up and run. She couldn't believe a

person could be having this conversation, especially with her mother-in-law. What did Minx expect her to say?

"You were both such babies," Minx went on. "When you were married, Julius didn't have a *clue*."

Well, he had more clues than I did, thought Liza, but she didn't say that. Everything had seemed to happen more or less as she'd expected. Although, come to think of it, what had she known? She still had the little old brown book that Minx had handed to her before their wedding. Liza knew just where it sat in the bookcase upstairs, turned backward on the shelf so Peggy Sue's mother wouldn't spot it when she came to babysit. The message of the book seemed remote: not just the Husband, but also the Wife, it said, was supposed to enjoy Married Love. The Husband must learn to be patient. This was the way to attain Perfect Happiness.

Minx lit another cigarette and stood up to walk around the room. For the first time, Liza wondered why Minx had offered the book to *her*. Julius had needed that lesson. And still did, if the truth be known.

Minx sat down again at the other end of the sofa. All of a sudden, Liza had the strangest urge to tell her about Derek. Minx might be the one person in all the world who would understand. You're crazy, she told herself, you can't do that.

The fire had sunk to red coals. Minx stubbed out her cigarette. Her glass was empty.

"Night-night, dearie." Smelling of whiskey, cigarettes, and faintly still her perfume, Minx hugged Liza at the door of her room. Liza hugged her back, feeling the bones of Minx's rib cage, fragile as glass.

Liza put out the lights on the Christmas tree, emptied her mother-in-law's ashtray, turned down the heat, and walked slowly up the stairs.

LIZA HAD her arms around a pillow from which she'd removed the case. Out the window she watched two red squirrels darting through the black leafless branches of the elm in front of the house. She and Abby had watched Minx go off with Julius that morning, two days after Christmas. Liza was relieved that Minx's visit was over, but now she felt let down. She pulled the sheets off the guest room bed and collected Minx's damp towels and overflowing wastebasket. Minx drives us crazy, she told herself. But still . . . she understands a lot of things Julius would never dream of. He'd think I'd lost my mind. I *have* lost my mind. And oh, my heart, too.

She turned when she heard the loud rattle of Abby's new toy dump truck rumbling into the room across the bare wood floor. Julius had given Abby this sturdy metal truck because he didn't think little girls should play just with dolls.

"Look, Mommy, look!"

Abby had squeezed her old doll, her new doll, and two stuffed rabbits into the back of the yellow truck. Liza laughed.

"Oh, they're all having a ride. Where are they going?"

"They came to see you."

After she'd started some laundry and picked up the cluttered kitchen, Liza stuffed Abby into her red snowsuit, and headed out the door.

"We have to get some milk, we have to go to the post office . . ."

Just as they were making their way down the front path, a small tan car whirled into the driveway. Derek's MG. Derek.

Liza felt a sudden wrench of happiness. I thought I might never see him again. Oh, what's going to happen? What *can* happen? She felt for a second as if she were watching a movie.

"Look, Mommy." Abby said, standing still. "Here comes Derek."

Derek climbed out of the car and came toward them. His face above his dark parka looked white, narrow, tense. He didn't smile. Bluish smoke from his cigarette rose straight up in the cold, still air.

"Hi," Liza said in a choked voice. "I thought . . . that I might not see you again."

"I want you to come to where they're starting to build the new highway."

"Now?"

"Yes."

They got into his car. Liza held Abby on her lap.

A new interstate was about to cut Rock Hill in half. The town selectmen were conferring with important officials from Boston, putting on suits and ties to be driven around town in shiny blue cars with cryptic logos. As to the exact route of the highway, rumors were rife: "Old man Wheeler's farm just might become *very valuable*," Chipper Reilly had muttered solemnly when Julius ran into him at the dump. As orange stakes began marching ominously through the town, some people complained when they realized their own street might become a dead end.

"Well, you can't stop progress!" said Mr. LaComb at the Atomic Super Market.

"This will put Rock Hill on the map, for sure," said Fran Headley the postmistress.

"Where are we going, Mommy?"

Liza talked softly to Abby and held her tight.

They turned into a broad dirt track that had recently been cut through old woods. The MG lurched and bounced over frozen ruts, past a line of mud-spattered pickup trucks. When they drew near to the construction site, Derek stopped. Liza carried Abby as they walked toward the painful grinding whine of chainsaws and the roar of monstrous vehicles. Every few minutes would bring the swish and thud of another tree crashing down. Abby burrowed into Liza's shoulder. "That dump truck looks just like yours," Liza said in a trembly voice into Abby's ear. Their voices were drowned by the noise. How small we are, Liza thought. She looked at Derek, so frail, suddenly so small.

Construction vehicles were working all along a wide swath of churned-up earth. As far as they could see in either direction, caterpillar tractors were bumping back and forth like monstrous crazed yellow beetles. Through the fringe of pines on the far side of the cut Liza could just see a white farmhouse and a red barn. Why, that's the Coxes' farm, she realized with a pang. A perfect farm, neat rows of apple trees . . . eternal.

Abby, clinging to Liza, couldn't take her eyes off the moving vehicles. An open jeep with an official insignia on its side pulled up and stopped near them. A man in a hard hat and mud-caked boots jumped out. "Can I help you folks?"

"We're just looking," Derek said.

"I wouldn't stand there if I were you. With the little girl and all. You never know when a branch might let go. Or a rock."

They turned and walked back toward Derek's car. "It sounded as if he were threatening us," Liza said.

"It's real, Liza. Look at that old wall — rocks scattered like marbles. And those big oaks . . ." He paused. "This is the beginning of the end of Rock Hill, you know. Dad and my grandfather used to hunt all through here. Farmers used to run cattle, raise hay, apples . . ."

They got into his car, but Derek didn't start it up right away. Liza watched his knuckles turn white as he gripped the steering wheel.

"I guess I'm part of the problem, Derek. Julius and me, people like us, outsiders coming in."

Derek looked at her. His hands dropped to his knees. "A lot of things are ending, Liza, but not you. I shouldn't have brought you here."

"Derek." Liza wanted to hold him tight, comfort him. But she had Abby in her arms. All she could do was lean toward him, put her head on his shoulder.

"Oh, Liza . . ." He put his arms around her and Abby for a long minute. Liza took long deep breaths. Derek's shirt, Derek himself, smelled like sun-warmed laundry off the line, like grass just cut. She felt his fingers firm against her back. She pressed her cheek into the hollow beneath his shoulder.

Then Abby squirmed, and Derek's arms fell away as he straightened up. He started to say something, but Abby spoke first. "Home now, Mommy. Home to Abby's house."

Derek laughed, a short bitter laugh. "Yes, Abby, I'll take you home right now."

"There's nothing for us, Derek. Isn't that true?" Through tears she looked at Derek's profile, his chin lifted, eyes looking far away. "I've been dreaming. We have to stop." She shook her head. She couldn't talk any more. Derek started the car.

"Mommy, don't cry."

When they pulled into her driveway, Liza was still choking back sobs. She opened the door and started to climb out.

"Wait a sec." Derek was reaching into a pocket of his parka. "Look Abby, these are for you."

He held two tiny metal elephants on his outstretched palm. "Watch what they do."

When he put the elephants side by side they jumped around until they stood trunk to trunk. He did it again.

Abby crowed with delight. "El-e-phants. Funny elephants."

Liza smiled. "Magnets?"

Derek put one elephant behind the other. Again they leapt and turned to face each other.

"They're for you, Abby. Do you remember when we went to see the big elephants?"

Abby nodded. "And Abby said, 'No ride.'" Liza smiled at the memory, smiled because Derek was so awkward with a child, and so sweet. But it could never happen again, she realized. The emptiness dropped through her like a weight.

Now Derek was fumbling in another pocket. He pulled out a small dark green book, handing it to Liza. She ran her hands over the soft leather, and opened it to the swirly wave-patterned endpapers and the creamy blank pages.

"Thank you. It's beautiful. What should I . . .?"

"Whatever you want. Bye, Abby; you're a nice girl." He looked at Liza, his mouth in a half smile. "G'bye, Liza. See you around."

"I *guess* so . . ." But this was goodbye. He climbed into the car and drove off. Abby and Liza waved.

"Oh, Abby." Liza sank down, burying her face in Abby's red snowsuit.

When she stood up she said, "Mummy forgot the milk." Hand in hand, they walked into their house.

EVVY CALLED up. She and Liza talked on the phone.

"We're going skiing at Mittersill this weekend," Evvy told her. "Ham's dad always makes a big deal out of New Year's Eve. It'll be a real bash, sort of crude, but, you know, fun."

Liza couldn't help wondering whether Derek would go to Mittersill, too. It didn't sound like him, but she wasn't going to ask Evvy.

Julius and Liza spent New Year's Eve at the Ryans'. Both Peggy Sue and her mother were busy that night, so they took Abby along. About nine o'clock Liza tucked her into bed beside Duane.

Billie hollered up from downstairs. "Duane! You take good care of Abby now, you hear? Don't you let that precious little baby fall out of the bed."

Abby's eyes were big with excitement. In the band of light from the door she lay straight and still. Liza whispered in her ear, "You have to be quiet as a mouse, sweetie, so Duane can go to sleep."

Downstairs, Tom and Julius talked as usual about politics. Billie Ray chimed in with more passion than either of them. She was still lamenting Adlai Stevenson's loss to Eisenhower.

"Ike's not so bad," Julius was saying. I mean, naturally I personally would *rather* have had Stevenson, but actually, in some ways . . ."

Billie cut him off. "You men, you're just the same! If Stevenson were in the White House, we would have *done* something about those brave Hungarians, the only ones who stood up to the Russians. I'm ashamed to be an American sometimes, I truly am."

"Oh, Billie's on a tear again," Tom said. "But she's right, as usual. How 'bout another beer, Jules?"

They talked about Hungary, French Indo-China, and the mess in Washington.

"Julius, you oughta get into some pro bono legal work," Tom said. "Sure, we have a great justice system, but what good is it for all the folks who can't afford a lawyer?"

"Hmm. Not sure how the firm would take to *that*."

"The new highway is finally happening," Liza said.

"Oh, I hate to see it," said Billie. "Rock Hill won't be the same quiet little old town when they get through."

"If it ever was," Tom said. "Well, the Cliffords must be happy, anyhow. A guy I know — he's a lawyer for the DPW — told me they landed the contract for all the granite curbing for the whole stretch, New Hampshire to the Rhode Island line."

"Whoa, that's a lot of granite," said Julius.

"Yeah, and the Cliffords still treat their workers like — scum."

"There'll be more people, more houses," Billie said.

"Rock Hill will be just like every place," said Liza.

Julius had brought champagne. Billie came in from the kitchen holding up a cake in front of her bosom.

"Ribbon cake," she said. "Seven layers. My Great Aunt Frankie's recipe."

Accident

LIZA AND Abby walked into the post office just after Fran Headley had unlocked the door.

"Happy New Year, Fran. Could I have a book of stamps?"

Fran looked glum. "I'm so upset about that poor boy, I can't think straight."

Peg Reilly came in. "Isn't it terrible? Chipper says he must have been drinking."

"What happened?" asked Liza. She stared at the faces of the two women.

"You didn't hear? The Clifford boy, the youngest. His car just went right off the road, Mammoth Road, where it makes that sharp bend. Killed right off, musta been."

Liza's mind was whirling. The room spun. Voices sounded far away. She squeezed Abby's hand as if for support.

"He was alone, anyhow. No one even heard the crash! Chief Gerrity was going by on the early shift, and just happened to see the car there in the trees, all crunched up.

Liza stood, remembering the hollow of his shoulder, his hands on the piano keys, on her back, the soft back of his neck. She inhaled as if she might recover the freshness of him.

From Abby's mittened hand the letters they'd brought for the mail fell to the floor in a perfect fan.

"Abby," Liza snapped. She bent down, scooped up the envelopes, and grabbed Abby's hand again, yanking at her as they pushed out the door, almost colliding with Ed Wells the selectman. As Liza turned she saw Fran Headley's moon face, her mouth an O, and Liza's forgotten stamps in her uplifted hand.

Liza lifted Abby and pushed her into the car seat, then slammed the door. Abby cried all the way home.

The sun was blinding, reflected off the snow, but the sky seemed dark. Liza stopped the car with a jerk when they got home. Now she began to cry, too. "Oh Abby, my poor darling, Mummy's sorry, Mummy's sad, Mummy loves you." Gently she pulled Abby onto her lap, hugging her, rocking to and fro, both of them gulping, both overwhelmed with woe.

They spent a long time in the rocking chair that morning, reading story after story — *Peter Rabbit, The Three Bears*, Babar grieving for his mother — while Wendell, his head on his paws, his brown eyes watching, seemed to listen and grieve, too. With a cookie cutter, Liza made Abby a cream cheese and jelly sandwich in the shape of a duck. After she put Abby down for her nap, Liza stood there in the hall, outside Abby's door, looking at nothing. After a minute or two her feet took her to the bedroom, where she fell onto the big bed. Remembered moments, images, ran like color slides through her head. She could *see* Derek in his clean white shirt, his gray eyes looking at her, looking far away.

Liza didn't move until at last she heard Abby calling. Then she couldn't do anything but sit at the kitchen table, patting the soft fur behind Wendell's ears and watching Abby with her stuffed rabbits. Later that afternoon she made herself a cup of tea. It's gone now, she thought, the possibility of joy, gone for good. That was what Derek gave me, the possibility of joy. And I didn't give him even that.

"I CAN'T believe it; they're not having a wake!" Peg Reilly seemed shocked by her own news when she ran into Liza at the Atomic Super Market two days after the accident. "Everything's going to be private."

In Rock Hill when a prominent old-timer died, everyone filed through Foote's Funeral Parlor, past the banked floral tributes and the open casket, and then hung around afterward signing the book and chatting. Liza had been to a few of these viewings when Julius thought they should make an appearance. Now she tightened her grip on the shopping cart. "Derek would have hated that," she said.

Peg's eyes widened. "Well. You're the one to know," she said, heading toward the frozen foods.

Minx telephoned. She talked to Liza. "I just heard about that awful accident. Dear Bunny Hopkins called me. That poor, poor boy, Derek. But I really wasn't surprised."

"Minx! What do you mean?"

"He had the look of doom. I could tell. It would have been something else if not this. His poor mother; I'll write her."

"It's really sad." This was the first time Liza had said even that.

"I know how you feel, dearie. You cared about him. I know."

How did she know, Liza wondered, but for the moment she felt comforted.

The days were long. Everything in her life seemed stale. She couldn't even bring herself to call Billie. Reading to Abby one afternoon, she missed a page in *Peter Rabbit*.

"You didn't tell the part about Peter's jacket getting caught on the fence!" Abby squirmed in Liza's lap, looking up at her. "Read it right, Mommy." Even Wendell's brown eyes were filled with reproach.

After the first days, Julius and Liza never mentioned the accident. Over dinner in their chaste modern kitchen, Liza would try to concentrate on what Julius was telling her.

"Mr. Pointer came to my desk, and said I'd done a good job with the Alden Worsted Company brief. He's head of the tax division, so, well, that was something. You know, for him to say that." He held his fork in midair, and looked expectantly at Liza.

"That's wonderful. Was that the case about the wind-up toys?"

Julius looked pained. He shook his head. "I don't think you were listening," but he said it gently.

Deep down, Liza had never really liked to cook. The only way she could make it interesting was to keep trying new dishes, from unusual meatloaf recipes Peg Reilly or Gladys Shoemaker passed on, or casseroles out of her *Take it Easy Before Dinner* cookbook, and complicated cakes of Billie's. But lately she had no heart for anything she had to think about. Now it was just hamburgers, rice, frozen peas. The next night, spam, baked potatoes, frozen corn. Dessert would be Breyers' chocolate ice cream or canned peach halves. If Julius noticed anything different, he never mentioned it.

The sun began to seem brighter in February, even when the thermometer outside the kitchen window hovered near zero.

"I was thinking maybe we should get away for a weekend," Julius said one day. "Spend a couple of nights in Boston, maybe the Parker House. Go to a play or something."

Liza was startled. She'd used to dream of doing exactly that, but now? She couldn't say no.

"I'll have to see if Peggy Sue's mother can come," Liza hedged. She saw Abby's eyes grow big. ". . . to take good care of Abby," she said, giving her a hug.

In Boston, they watched a new English movie at the Exeter Theater. They went to Brooks Brothers to buy some black socks for Julius. Liza bought herself Graham Greene's newest novel, *The Quiet American*, and read half the night, while Julius snored gently in the other bed. In the morning, they had French toast for breakfast in their room. The weekend went well, as well as Liza had expected.

Egg Man

THAT SPRING, for the first time, Julius began practicing a little bit of law in Rock Hill. If you could call it law; Liza wasn't sure. It was more like marriage counselling. It started with eggs. One night, at a Mr. & Mrs. Club meeting, Peg Reilly said, "Liza, you ought to try Mr. Jobe's eggs. He delivers right to the door, they're fresh, and they're actually cheaper than at the Atomic!"

"Oh, I didn't know."

"The way I figure it, he saves us from having to keep hens. We used to, of course, but oh my! Raccoons, foxes, I don't know what all got after them. My Melanie would come in every morning, crying her little heart out. Pitiful."

So Mr. Jobe would stop by the Prescotts on Tuesday afternoons with a dozen eggs. Wendell would bark, and Mr. Jobe would say, "Down boy," as if he knew it was hopeless. Liza would hand him the box from the week before, along with forty cents. Mr. Jobe had very little chin or forehead, but he did have a wing of pale orange hair that would flop back when he looked up at Liza. They didn't talk much, and Wendell never got over barking whenever Mr. Jobe tried to come up the front walk.

One Tuesday, after a few weeks, Mr. Jobe said, "Would you be interested in a fresh-killed hen for your pot?" He just happened to have a nice one in the truck.

Liza cooked the hen all day, until the water had boiled away. At dinner Julius said, "It's like eating rubber bands."

Liza laughed. "No more hens from Mr. Jobe!"

A week or two later, Mr. Jobe said, "Do you suppose I could talk with your hubby some night? Having a few legal problems."

"He doesn't really do much work at home . . ." — a lie, Liza told herself; Julius spends half his life working on stuff out of that fat old briefcase —"but I'll ask him."

"A little community work wouldn't hurt, I guess," Julius said later. He called Mr. Jobe to set a time.

After that, every Thursday they'd rush through dinner before Mr. Jobe appeared on their doorstep at seven-fifteen. Julius would close the study door, but Liza, upstairs with Abby and working on her needlepoint, could hear their voices for the next hour or so. The eggs still came on Tuesdays as usual.

"What's his problem?" Liza asked Julius.

"The grain dealer's after him; he owes them a *lot*. And Mrs. Jobe isn't being very cooperative. Plus their oldest boy's in trouble, threatening kids with knives, setting little fires."

"Oh dear," Liza said. "That doesn't sound like legal stuff."

"Well, what can I do? He gave me five dollars the first time, but I'm not going to take any more."

"Julius, you're good."

One evening, not a Thursday, their dinner was interrupted by a knock at the door, and fierce barks from Wendell. Liza opened it to find a little wiry woman with a pinched face, still wearing a dotted bib apron over her faded blue housedress.

"You don't know me. I'm Mrs. Jobe." She had to raise her voice above Wendell. "Sorry to bother, but I have to see Mr."

Julius showed her into the study and closed the door.

This is getting out of hand, Liza said to herself as she cleaned up the kitchen.

It got worse. Soon both Jobes were coming over together to talk to Julius. Upstairs, Liza would put her hands over her ears when she heard their loud angry voices.

"I'm the one does all the plucking, all the gutting," shrilled Mrs. Jobe. "While he's out, all gussied up, delivering stuff to pretty ladies. I'm telling you . . ."

It got so Julius dreaded Thursday nights. And there were phone calls in between.

"I finally got the grain people to agree to a *little* payment every week," Julius told Liza. "But now Jobe won't even do that. I tried to persuade the guy to give his wife a hand, but . . . aagh, it's hopeless."

Early one Saturday, before Liza had even made the coffee, they heard the town fire alarm in the distance and the shriek of sirens. An hour later, Julius was loading their trash into the station wagon for his weekly run to the town dump. Liza and Abby were outside when he got home.

"Well, guess what," he said. "That was Jobe's henhouse that burned. Set, according to Chief Gerrity. No doubt about it."

"How terrible," Liza said, her hands at her cheeks. "Now what?"

A maroon Chevrolet swung into their driveway. It was Gladys and Skip Shoemaker.

"Have you folks heard the news?" Skip called from the car window. Skip was a volunteer fireman.

"Yeah, we heard."

"I was worried sick about Skip." Gladys said, as they clambered out of their car. "Hi Abby, little sweetheart." Abby clung to Liza's leg.

"Smelt like Thanksgiving over there. Roasted birds. We saved the house, but it's empty. Cleaned out. Jobes are *gone*."

"Can you beat that? Don't know what we'll do for eggs," said Gladys. "Those five kids. I had their Doreen in my Brownie troop. Sweet little thing, but too advanced, if you know what I mean." She turned to Liza. "Language," she mouthed.

After the Shoemakers finally left, Liza began fixing egg salad sandwiches for lunch. She put Abby in her high chair.

"Where will they go, do you think? And what can they do?" Liza was profoundly upset by her image of the Jobes: desperate, rootless, and homeless.

"I just hope they'll get away. Make a fresh start." Julius shrugged, but he looked sad and spent. "I tried, anyhow."

Liza put down a spoon and the mayonnaise jar. She whirled around and flung her arms around Julius, pressing her face against him. "You did, you did."

"Don't cry, Mummy." Abby's crumpled face looked as though she might cry.

Julius held Liza, and with his other arm, patted Abby on the head.

"Don't worry, darling. Everything will be all right."

Liza thought he might have been talking to her. It seemed possible.

Making Further Progress

"HAVEN'T SEEN you and Julius at Mr. & Mrs. Club lately," Peg Reilly said one day when she spotted Liza at the post office. "You should come Thursday. Just social, no speaker, and a new couple in town, the Fields."

"We've been busy," Liza said, "This and that, but I'll ask Julius."

Julius thought they should go, just to keep in touch. It was only once a month. Most of the important people in town — the younger ones, anyhow — belonged to Mr. & Mrs. Tom and Billie had gone twice, but never again. "I've got better ways to waste time," said Tom, who read De Toqueville on the train in the morning and brought work home every night.

Liza took her special Swedish meatballs to the Thursday meeting. She and Julius were early. Julius and Skip Shoemaker unrolled white paper onto the long tables in the church basement while Liza and Doris Gerrity, the police chief's wife, arranged casseroles and salads on the serving counter.

"You folks are friendly with the Cliffords, right?" Doris asked.

Liza hesitated. "Well, we know them." I *don't* want to talk about the Cliffords, she thought, clutching a stack of plates.

"The Pigeon-eer's fancy, I bet. They're so wealthy. I picture formal, maroon velvet and all."

"Well it's not formal, really, but pretty big." Liza tried to think of a detail that would satisfy Doris so she could get away. "*Two* fireplaces in the living room. Excuse me a sec."

"Terrible about their son . . ." Hearing Doris's voice

pursuing her, Liza winced as she fled toward the kitchen. I didn't hear, she told herself.

Couples were arriving in a steady stream.

"The Higginses couldn't make it," Skipper was saying. "Bernice called Gladys. They've had a time, what with their barn floor collapsing and all. Wood just rotted. When we got there with the fire truck, the cows were just dangling from the stanchions, all four hoofs in the air, just about. But we got 'em down; didn't lose a one."

Pearl Swanson introduced Liza and Doris to someone new. "Gals, this is Dawnette Fields. She and her hubby Rex have bought the Perkins's old farm."

Dawnette was blonde and curvy, in a royal blue sheath dress that went with her shadowed eyes and blue lashes. "We're restoring it," she said.

Restoring it to what? Liza wondered.

Pearl led Dawnette off to meet more people.

"A bottle blonde, if ever I saw one," Doris muttered.

Liza spotted Rex Fields — definitely a newcomer — surrounded by Chipper Reilly, Spider, and Julius. Rex was tall, dark, and movie-star handsome, if you like that sort of thing, thought Liza. Bronzed face: he must work outside.

They didn't have anything *first* at the Mr. & Mrs. meetings, no alcohol, of course — it being a church — so as soon as everyone had assembled, they lined up for the buffet. Husbands and wives always sat together, naturally. Once Tilly Follen had raised eyebrows, sitting down next to Puggy Swenson and talking to him. But she learned. Julius steered Liza toward the new couple.

"So. Where are you from, Rex?" Julius asked.

"Been in construction all my life," Rex said. "Working for my dad, out around Brimfield area. Decided it was time to strike out, didn't we, hon?" He turned toward Dawnette, who simpered. Rex was wearing a black shirt made of some shiny material, with silver cufflinks. Liza was reminded of the enemy Fascists in the War, not a nice memory.

"Yeah," Rex went on. "When we hit on Rock Hill, we knew it was right. Real sleepy little place, but so much going for it, with the new highway and all."

Liza had a sinking feeling. She sat up straight. "So what will you be doing?"

"Not to worry," Rex said. "We're homebuilders. Rex Fields, Inc., nice ranch homes for folks like you." He grinned at her, showing all his white teeth.

"Hmmph," said Julius. Probably no one had ever built more than one house at a time in Rock Hill.

"That's progress for you," said Chipper Reilly from across the table.

Skip Shoemaker chimed in. "Yep, can't stop progress."

"Rock Hill will be on the map now, that's for sure," shrilled Gladys Shoemaker.

"Oh, I'm starting small." Rex Fields's face was sober. "It's just vacant land, near my house. Not good for anything much. It'll be beautiful when we're done."

Liza stared at Rex, thinking, that's where I walked those mornings, behind the library. Those fields, the woods, the stone walls. Derek. Her eyes filled, and she looked at the ceiling.

"That land is beautiful *now*." Liza sounded as fierce as she felt.

Everyone looked at her. "The future's coming," Julius said. The men all nodded their heads, even though you couldn't really tell what Julius meant.

Dawnette Fields never said a word. Her placid blue gaze rested easily on her husband.

Across the room, Peg Reilly clapped her hands. "Dessert time! Come and get it, guys, gals." With a great noise of chairs being pushed back, club members lined up in front of three-layer chocolate cakes, puffed-up apple pies, and lemon pies with thick swirls of meringue on top.

"I'M OFF to the dump," Julius told Liza one Saturday morning. "Want to come along? I was thinking we could drive past Rex Fields's new houses after, see what he's up to."

He loaded three dented galvanized trash cans into the back of the station wagon. Liza held Abby on her lap in the front seat. She rolled up her window when they turned into the town dump, but foul smoke and dust blew in through the open tailgate. Liza laid her palm over Abby's face, as if to protect her.

"Ugh," Liza said. "It stinks."

"Enough dump," Abby said. "Home now."

But Julius was deep in conversation with Duke Handegun, the dump keeper, and Spider Follen, who'd happened to drive in at the same time.

Finally Julius came back to the car, wearing a smile that didn't show his teeth. "This is the place to get the news," he said. "According to Duke, they had to take Alice Parlee to the nursing home. Looks like we're going to need a new town clerk."

"Oh, dear. But what about *Lilly?*" Lilly, a huge English sheepdog, was Alice's sole companion, a friendly dog, fortunately, who wagged her tail at people trying to thread their way through the piled-up boxes and overflowing paper bags on Alice's sagging sunporch to register their own dogs or pick up a marriage license.

"Someone was over there, looking for Alice, and they heard moaning from upstairs. So whoever it was called the police. The chief drove Lilly over to Mrs. Barnwell's kennel. She'll be fine."

"And how about *Alice?*" Liza heard her voice sounding shrill.

"You asked me about Lilly. Well, Alice had had some sort of attack, I guess. She couldn't get out of bed."

Spider had ambled over to lean in the window of their car. "She didn't even know what day it was. I was in there last week, and there was Alice all dolled up sitting at the table, poking through a bowl of cornflakes with those long pink fingernails of hers. I said, 'What's up, Alice?' 'Dropped my false eyelashes,' that's what she said, and I believe it."

"That's awful." Liza didn't mean to laugh. "Well," she paused. "Maybe I'll have to take over her job. If she's really sick, I mean." I could, she thought, I really could. It was as if a light had come on.

"Don't be ridiculous," Julius said. "And you shouldn't say things like that anyway, when a person's sick." But Liza hardly heard him. She was looking out the window, thinking about changing her life.

Abby turned to look up at Liza. "She didn't have any spoon? That lady?" Her eyes were wide with worry.

"What? What do you mean, Abby?"

"Liza, we were talking about Alice Parlee. Of course she had a spoon, honey."

"Yes, my sweet, she had a spoon, but now she's sick." Liza smoothed back blonde wisps and kissed Abby's forehead, "But she'll be fine, don't you worry."

Empty trash cans clanked in the back of the car as Julius drove out from the smoky dump onto the blacktop road. When they were halfway down Quarry Hill they saw a big sign and a new road off to the right. Julius turned in and stopped. He read aloud: "Boots 'N Saddles. Fine Homes." The sign included a picture of a ten-gallon hat and a little site plan. They studied the plan.

"Well, right this minute we are on Rodeo Road at Corral Circle," said Julius in a somber tone.

"I can't believe it," cried Liza. "This looks like a city, all these streets."

"How about the names? Mustang Drive, Buckboard Lane . . ."

"Maverick Way," added Liza. "And ranch houses, naturally." The new light poles made her think of rifles.

On this Saturday morning the future street was empty. Julius drove slowly past the sprawling, half-built houses. Around the first bend the dusty rutted road came to a temporary halt, but the devastated woodland beyond was littered with downed trees, piles of leafy brush, and blown paper.

Nothing that Liza saw looked familiar from the walks she'd taken there. It was a different place. "I hate that Rex Fields," she said. She pictured him as a masked bandit, riding into town, scaring people, stealing beauty, stealing her sweet memories.

"Hate Rex Fields," echoed Abby.

"*Mr.* Fields, honey," said Julius. "You know who's the silent partner, Liza. Or maybe you don't? It's old man Clifford. He's a businessman; he sees the handwriting . . ."

Liza shut her eyes for a long moment. She remembered how it had looked when she'd walked across that field with Derek. She fingered the white stone, still in her coat pocket. He would have fought this, she told herself; he would, he would. But she knew he would have lost that battle, too.

"I hate this," she moaned, covering her eyes. "Let's *go*."

Julius talked to Abby as he drove them home. "We'll come back when the men are working, Abby. We'll see all the big machines go."

Liza let her chin sink into Abby's soft fair hair.

Two to One

On Monday morning, a week later, Liza went with Abby up to the town hall. Their feet sounded like hammers as they walked hand in hand down the bare boards of the long empty hallway.

"Well howdy, Mrs. Prescott," said Charlie, the selectmen's wizened, white-haired secretary, leaning across his brown wooden counter. "And my, what a pretty little girl. Aren't you, sweetheart?"

"Charlie, I'd like to apply for the town clerk job." Liza could feel her heart beating fast.

Charlie stared. "Hunh. Is that so? You know Alice Parlee worked out of her house, no office or nothing. You wouldn't be wanting all that in *your* house, would you?"

"I'd have to work in *her* house for a while. You know, all those piles of boxes and papers, the file cabinets — and all I've ever seen was the room where she worked that must have been a dining room once. And who knows how much town stuff she had in all the other rooms? Someone's got to go through it all."

"How about this little lady?" Charlie patted Abby's blonde head. "Who's going to mind her if Mommy goes out to work?"

Guilt was already making Liza's stomach tight. She put her arm around Abby. "Tell the man how old you are, Abby."

Without speaking, Abby held up four fingers.

"And what does Julius think of all this, his wife going off to take a job?"

Liza brushed away an imaginary fly. She put both elbows on the counter. "Charlie, how do I apply? Is there a form or something? Or should I just come to the selectmen's meeting?"

Julius had a school committee meeting every Monday, so that night they had a quick early dinner of hamburgers and frozen corn. As Julius was gathering up his papers and gulping his coffee, almost ready to race out the door, Liza said, "I'll be going out tomorrow night, Julius." She tried to swallow.

"Oh? To Billie Ray's?"

"No. To the selectmen's meeting. I've decided to apply for the town clerk's job."

Julius stopped at the door, his mouth open. Liza felt a surge of pity, of love, of regret. She stood up, heading toward him, her hands uplifted. "Don't worry, Julius . . ."

"I've gotta go." He shook his head, brushing Liza away. "We'll talk tomorrow." Then he was off, striding down the path, shoulders hunched, head poking forward, to his car.

Liza sank back in her chair, closed her eyes, and took great gulps of air.

The selectmen voted two to one in favor of hiring Liza, with Patti Foote opposed. "As a Mom myself, I think she should be home with her baby."

But Liza had her own opinions about Patti Foote, her dancing school, and the silly way she flirted and who-knew-what-else with every man she saw, including Rex Fields. She drove home, floating on a cloud. Julius had left one light on for her, at the foot of the stairs. She tiptoed into their dark bedroom.

"I got the job, Julius." She laid her hand on the long narrow mound in the bed.

"Umm." He turned over. "What?" When he understood, he sat up. "Mmm. That's good."

"Sorry I woke you up."

"No, it's fine, it's okay." He lay down again.

Liza undressed for bed, but was too excited to sleep.

A Silent House

FOR FOUR mornings a week Liza waded through the masses of paper in Alice Parlee's house. Abby stayed at home, looked after by Peggy Sue during the summer, and in the fall went happily off to nursery school, along with Thurman and Donny Ryan.

At first, Liza had dreaded unlocking Alice's door and walking into that silent house, an intact artifact of Victorian days with a dense overlay of more recent clutter. She found keys to Alice's four clocks and set them all ticking. From one of them would come, every hour, a little whir, followed by a sweet clear chime. As time went on, Liza developed a system for sorting the jumbled papers: marriage licenses here, death notices there, dogs in that file, voting lists in this one. It was soothing and satisfying to bring order out of chaos, like reorganizing Julius's sock drawer. But it was more than that. Liza knew it was important work, keeping track of a whole town. She had no one to talk to about it. Once Julius had gotten used to the idea, he began to take her new job for granted. Billie kept saying, "How can you stand that dirty old place, all by yourself?" And Evvy would dismiss Liza's job with one word: "Boring."

Only two or three times a week did anyone disturb the quiet — a new voter once in a while, or a clean and serious young couple wanting a marriage license. A man she didn't know — one of Rock Hill's prolific Gerrity clan — came one day to fill the oil tank in the cellar. The town was paying the oil bills until the house was sold.

"Ever get lonesome up here all by yourself? Just you let me know if you want some company," he smirked, and stood there holding the end of the fuel hose for a long minute.

Liza leaned forward, pretending to study the papers she

held. Her stomach muscles were tight as she counted, praying until he left.

Months later, after Liza had gone through the files in the dining room — more recently Alice's office — she moved through other musty rooms, and finally the hot, cobwebbed attic. She found brittle cartons of papers from World War I, names of draftees, influenza warnings, casualty lists. Other boxes held tax record books from the last century. She turned the yellowed pages of selectmen's longhand minutes and town meeting votes going back to the 1880s. Once — she couldn't help it — she thumbed through town reports until she found it: Derek Mills Clifford, born April 18, 1933. Twenty-five he'd be now, she thought. And I never even knew his birthday.

On her way to Alice's house in the morning, she'd wonder what she would find that day; it was like a treasure hunt. Every now and then she'd pause, sit back, and reflect on what she was doing, or trying to do. What is this all about, she'd ask herself sometimes in the middle of the night, in bed at home. Nobody except me knows what's there, and I may be the only one who cares. But these are peoples' lives, and now part of their history is being bull-dozed away. It matters.

An Unexpected Payoff

LIZA PUT her first paycheck in her wallet and carried it around for a week. Every now and then she'd pull it out just to look. It was nearly four times as much as she paid Peggy Sue, and three times what she'd earned waiting on tables on Nantucket one summer.

"How are you ever going to get all your preserving done?" Gladys Shoemaker asked Liza one day when they met at the Atomic Market. "What with spending all your time up at Alice's."

"Don't you get spooked by that crazy old house?" Peg Reilly chimed in. "Myself, I couldn't stand being up there, and all alone."

"Abby, honey, I bet you miss your mama." Gladys leaned over to pat Abby's head.

"I cooked *brownies* for Mommy! Peggy Sue helped."

Liza smiled. "They were the best brownies I ever had, Abby. My favorite, with nuts." She and Abby headed for the check-out.

"Some people in this town are so nasty," Liza told Julius that night. "Especially the women. Gladys and Peg try to make me feel guilty: neglecting Abby, supposedly, and not freezing enough beans or making enough jam."

"Aagh, don't listen to those old witches. What do they know? I'm really proud of you."

"You *are*?" Liza, open-mouthed, swivelled toward him. "You never said that before."

They were sitting in Julius's study after dinner, after Abby was asleep. Liza had read a Babar book to Abby, sung "Gaily Sings the Donkey," as usual, and "Tender Shepherd" twice.

"But Julius, seriously," Liza said, when she had collected herself, tamped down her joy. "What should I do with all this town stuff, besides cataloguing it, I mean? After all, it's *history*."

"That's it. It is history, and you should write it. How long has it been since that old "History of Rock Hill" was written?"

Liza turned to pull their copy out of the bookcase. "1868. That's . . . ninety years ago."

"Yes, and by the time you finish it'll be close to a hundred."

"Julius, do you really think I could? I'd love to try; I'm hooked already, but . . ."

"I *know* you can."

Liza wiggled her toes when she thought about Julius praising her. And lately he seemed to find her interesting in other ways, too. Sometimes now he'd come up and put his arms around her, press his face against her hair. "Julius," she'd say, laughing while he blew in her ear. At night, if he were reading in bed, he'd sometimes put aside his book when she came in, fresh and fragrant from her bath.

One Sunday morning, as she sat up in bed, reaching for her towel bathrobe, she looked at Julius, indolent, with his pajama top unbuttoned. "Maybe . . . Julius, maybe it's time that we had a hook on our door, on the inside. Just sometimes. What do you think?"

"Mmm, yes. Definitely. But later." He reached out toward her across the bed.

No Easy Cure

MRS. BOND, who ran Abby's little nursery school, recommended a book to Liza. "Abby's been asking questions, and I think it would be better coming from you at home."

"Oh? Already?" Liza was mortified that she might have neglected her responsibility. She hurried to the library to check out *The Wonderful Story of How You Were Born.*

"Ah, the birds and the bees," murmured Miss Bynum the librarian, with a thin smile.

Liza didn't respond. "Thank you," she said

On page one was a dot, a period. "That's how big you were, Abby."

By the end of the book the dot had grown into a whole baby, curled up into a round ball. The last page was the most exciting because you finally got to see the Mummy and Daddy, standing side by side, smiling down at a be-ribboned basket, from which a tiny hand seemed to be waving frantically.

"Aah!" Liza burst out. "The Mommy and the Daddy are really important, Abby. But you'd never know it from this book."

That was enough for one day. Abby looked at that book every day until they had to take it back to the library.

Julius and Tom Ryan took turns taking the children to nursery school, while Liza drove them home. Billie still had no car most days, and besides, she was pretty tied down with Desmond, the new baby. Sometimes she'd invite Liza and Abby to stay for lunch.

"Desmond's my sweetest baby yet, aren't you, precious?" Billie cradled him at her breast. "I love them best when they're new, so helpless and innocent. I guess that's what I was meant to do, have babies." Then she looked up at Liza. "Oh honey, I didn't mean to make you feel bad." She reached her hand out to Liza's arm.

A year ago Liza would have felt like crying, but now she didn't. Instead, she found herself telling Billie about the conference she was going to.

"It's in Maine, Bowdoin College. Three nights I'll be gone. Peggy Sue's mother is coming on Thursday. Julius says he'll take care of Abby over the weekend. He offered! I can't believe I'm actually going."

"Donny? Thurman!" Billie called from her rocker where she still sat, nursing her little blue bundle. "Be nice now, and share. Remember Abby's a little lady, she's not used . . . Forgive me, Liza honey, I didn't quite get what you were saying."

"Well, it's a Local History conference, all people in that field. Some of the top names are coming, men I really want to meet . . ."

"Try this banana bread, Liza." With Desmond in her arms, Billie brought Liza a cup of tea, and flipped open another Pepsicola for herself. She'd laid slices of banana bread on one of her old blue willow plates. "It's a new recipe, with sour cream."

A tremor in her voice made Liza look up. She was startled to see a tear slide over the curve of Billie's cheek onto the blue flannel bundle that was Desmond. "What's wrong? You're . . . upset."

Sinking into the rocker, Billie said, "Oh, Liza, you're so smart. I could never do something like that, even if I wanted to! Never, never." Billie rocked and rocked.

Liza heard herself mumbling platitudes, all the things Billie could do that she couldn't, on and on. She put her arms around Billie's shaking shoulders, but knew that for Billie there was no easy cure.

Wreck Room

"THE SHOEMAKERS have invited us to a party next Saturday. Just casual, Gladys said, maybe a cook-out, if it's nice. They want to show off their new rec room."

"Wreck room?" Julius frowned. "What the hell kind of room is that?"

"Well you know, in their basement."

"Come on in!" read a crayoned sign at the Shoemakers' door. "We're Down in the Rec Room." Julius and Liza had pulled into the driveway right behind Pearl and Puggy Swenson. Together they walked single file down the cellar stairs. The Reillys were there, of course, and Spider and Tilly, Erford and Mildred, plus the new couple, Rex and Dawnette Fields.

"Hi, how ya doin'?" Everyone was talking at once.

"Long time, no see."

"Cute shoes. New?"

"Hey there, fella," with a slap on the back.

"Looking good."

"Love your hair."

"I had to box in all the asbestos pipes," Chip Shoemaker was saying. "A lot of work, that's for sure."

"Wow, that's quite some bar," Julius said. "Mirrors and all — even the brass rail. Neat."

Dawnette was perched on one of the high bar stools, with her skirt maybe accidentally hiked up so that you could see a ribbon of white skin above the gartered top of a golden tan nylon. Liza watched Julius's eyes flick back and forth, following for a minute or two the mesmerizing swing of Dawnette's shiny red high-heeled pump.

"Hey, Julius. Name your poison," said Chipper. "And

Liza? Some of the ladies are checking out my Grasshoppers; real smooth. How does that sound?"

Gladys had spread red-checked plastic over the ping-pong table. "Try these Dilly Carrots," she said, offering a cut glass dish heaped with orange spears. "They're new; got it out of *McCall's*. Chipper hauled in bushels of carrots from the garden, and I had to do something! Twenty-three jars of them, so help yourself."

The men were clustered around the TV, an endless football game.

"How did you get your TV set into the wall like that?" asked Liza.

"Well, you know Chipper. Nothing's too much trouble."

By that time Chipper had on his chef's hat and a cute apron with a picture on the front of a man in a chef's hat and an apron, wielding, as Chipper was, a long-handled fork. He stood over a built-in grill just outside the sliding glass door.

"Prime sirloin, I want you to know. Look at that, two inches thick — and tender! Who wants theirs really rare? Ah, Spider, here you go. That'll put hair on your chest, just kidding."

"Come and get it, all you guys and gals," Gladys called. "Everything's homegrown, even the hash browns. Except the beef."

"That's a joke, son," said Spider in a growly voice.

"How 'bout that," Puggy said over a heaped plateful as he lumbered toward the TV.

Clutching her plate, Liza found a place on the sofa between Peg and Mildred.

"I froze so many beans this year," Mildred was saying. "Don't know how we'll ever get through them, just Erford and me, now the kids are gone."

"It was a good year for corn," Peg said. "Fifty-three quarts. Nice to have it all done — and you can do so much with corn."

"How about you, Liza? Finished all your freezing?"

197

"I didn't do much this year — just some peas and a batch of jelly from the wild grapes on our wall. We love that wild taste."

"No pies? We couldn't get through the winter without our pies. Next year we'll get you out blueberrying, now Abby's old enough."

"Well, listen," exclaimed Mildred. "Liza's a career gal now, don't forget, much too busy to do like we all do."

Liza saw the women's heads swivel toward her, tight scarlet lips making a slash across each face. Liza kept her head up and stared right back. She thought about the Local History conference she was going to the weekend after next, up at Bowdoin. That would really shock them. But naturally she didn't mention it, it was her secret.

"BILLIE INVITED us over for the Fourth. I said OK." Liza was putting out their coffee cups for the morning. Julius was having his glass of milk before bed.

"Hmm. Well, sure, we might as well. What time?" Julius always liked to be sure about time.

"She said around two or two-thirty."

"Two or two-thirty! What is that supposed to mean? Is this lunch or dinner or *what*?"

"I don't know, but don't worry; we'll be well fed. You know Billie. The Cliffords are going, too."

"Oh. Hmm. I wouldn't have expected that." Julius sounded more enthusiastic when he learned that Ham and Evvy would be there, too.

"Abby darling, come give me a hug." Billie, swathed in white gauzy folds, held out her arms. She was sitting on one of the straight chairs from the kitchen, out on the burnt patchy grass behind her house in the thin shade of two desiccated elms. Tom Ryan had set out a circle of chairs from the house, but everyone except Billie was standing. Evvy and Ham and little E had driven in just behind Julius and Liza.

Billie looks too big for her chair, Liza thought, especially when she scooped Abby onto her lap. Duane Ryan, now ten, her pale face pinched and serious, stood straight and tall beside her mother. With her faded blue shorts, and skinny legs longer than the whole rest of her, she is not at *all* like her mother, Liza thought. Liza was reminded of her ten-year-old self.

"So Ham, I wouldn't have expected you guys to be in town for the Fourth. Great to see you," Julius said.

"Well, no hunting, no skiing. Nothing to make life worthwhile." Ham turned to Billie. "Just kidding." Billie smiled blandly, not showing her teeth. Julius was the only one who laughed.

"Well, actually," Ham went on, "I'm not that crazy about the beach . . . and we *are* going to the Adirondacks next week, trout fishing with Dad. Catch a few big ones." Ham's eyes were hidden behind brown aviator glasses. Evvy wore brown-tinted glasses, too, Liza noticed, but hers swept up like wings on either side of her face.

Liza didn't like this conversation. The Ryans never went anywhere, as far as she knew. "It's hot," she said, pushing back her heavy moist hair.

Then they heard a far-off whistle. "Train! Train coming." Thurman and Donny Ryan scampered to the rail fence, with E following on his stumpy legs and Abby after him. The track, fringed with daisies and Queen Anne's Lace, with green hills beyond, ran right behind the Ryans' house. Only once every week or two did a freight train rattle by.

Liza loved the familiar train sounds: the mournful whistle, the rumbling getting louder, coming closer. Thurman and Donny waved wildly to the engineer. Everyone was watching as the empty cars clattered past. Liza read the names on the battered cars: Chicago & Western, Bangor & Aroostook, Atlantic Coastline, Chesapeake & Ohio — she thought of far-off places, miles of track. They all waved when the faded red caboose rattled by, and cheered when they saw an arm wave back. Liza looked over at Duane, holding up her thin arm. Only her fingertips moved, and just once. The train sounds faded. One more whistle, already far off.

"OK, OK, gang." Tom tossed a football to Julius. "Come on Evvy, Liza. Duane, you can play. Come on Thurman."

No one urged Billie to play. She sat, holding her baby, Desmond, just three months old. Abby stood beside her.

"Watch out for E," called Liza. E Clifford was in the middle of the game.

"Don't worry," Evvy panted, as she made a running pass to Tom. "He's a tough little kid, aren't you E?"

Duane caught the ball and stood holding it, paralyzed, her eyes wide.

"Here, Duane, toss it to me." Julius darted close to her with his hands open. Duane, turning pink, let the ball go.

After a while Ham threw a long pass toward Tom. Tom leapt up to catch it, then fell, landing on his back. Everyone gathered around him.

"Hey, I'm OK." But he didn't get up right away.

"Tom?" Billie called from her chair.

"It's OK." Tom sat up, and then stood, leaning on Julius. He hobbled back toward Billie and the house. With her hand, Liza brushed grass and dirt off the back of his white T-shirt.

Julius and Ham laid planks over sawhorses while Tom, looking pale and uncomfortable in the lone Adirondack chair, made suggestions. In the kitchen, fragrant with roasting meat, Liza asked Billie what she could do to help. Evvy filled a tin washtub with ice for the beer while Liza set out lemonade for the little ones and ice tea that Billie Ray had made in the sun. They filled two big tan mixing bowls with potato salad.

"Evvy, Liza tells me you two were at college together. You just finished when? Oh you girls are so young . . ." Billie sighed as she spooned pepper jelly into a glass dish.

"How was that conference, Liza?" Evvy asked. "Aren't you just back? Did you meet any dazzling men?"

Evvy was the only person who'd asked about the conference at Bowdoin. Julius had been more interested in telling Liza about his first ever expedition to the Atomic Super Market with Abby than in paying attention to what Liza had tried to tell him.

"Oh, it was great. We had wonderful lectures and discussions. Everyone was pretty serious; I learned a lot. Yes, there were some really nice men, interesting guys. Women, too. We're planning to stay in touch."

Liza said no more about her mountaintop experience, what heaven it had been to talk for hours, to stay up late, to linger over meals with people who seemed to appreciate *her*, including, it was true, a couple of men who would sit beside her during lectures or over coffee, and then at night walk her back to the women's dorm.

Evvy said, "Too bad you had to drop out of needlepoint lessons. I'm already starting my second chair seat."

Liza arranged salads and serving spoons down the center of the long table on the scorched lawn. There was a chair, a stool, or a wooden box for everyone. When Thurman saw his mother, holding a heavy steaming platter, come teetering down the back steps on heeled pumps, he shouted "Yay!" and banged on the table with his spoon. Billie exhaled a vast sigh as she put down a crackly brown turkey on a thick white platter in front of Tom.

"You roasted a *turkey*?" Julius looked stunned.

"Oh, you don't know Billie Ray," Tom said. "She doesn't just wait for Thanksgiving."

"Don't you want me to carve, Tom?" Ham asked.

"No, no, I'm OK. Honey . . ." Tom looked to Billie. "why does he look so . . . sunken? A lean and hungry turkey."

"Sweetie, it's *summer*! This is a summer turkey." Billie didn't seem abashed. "No one wants all that hot dressing and gravy in the summertime. It's the Fourth of July!"

I would cry for a week if I were Billie, thought Liza.

The children banged their forks on their white plates, imitating Thurman. "Hush," Duane said, putting her long pale fingers over Thurman's blunt ruddy ones.

Drunk with fatigue and food and the heat, after sponge cake and watermelon and spitting seeds at each other, the children struggled one after the other to a grassy spot in the shadow of the box-like garage. E staggered after them, leading with his fat stomach. He'd popped a button from the strap of his short-alls, and his face was rosy with melon juice. He collapsed on the grass with the others.

"He loves me, he loves me not." Duane plucked petals from a daisy. Thurman, Donny, and Abby, breathing heavily, tried to imitate her with black-eyed susans. "Loves me, loves me not." E clambered to his feet and began snatching off daisy heads. "Wuv, wuv me . . ."

Billie nursed her baby discreetly, veiled by layers of thin white fabric. Tom looked half asleep in the only comfortable chair. Julius, sprawled on his back in the grass, maybe was asleep. Liza was still perched on her straight kitchen chair, and the Cliffords shared a plaid blanket, side by side, not touching. Evvy was idly weaving dandelions into a chain.

Liza was wearing the flared yellow shorts she'd had ever since the summer she turned sixteen. She looked down at the flowers printed on the front; they made it look as if she were wearing a little apron. She'd always loved these shorts, and didn't think she'd ever had a bad time when she wore them. They were from another place, another life. That was the real Liza, she thought. She was glad the shorts were still here, and that she was still her same size. Maybe I still *am* that same Liza: it felt like a revelation.

Ham sat up suddenly. Now Duane had a red hula hoop around her narrow hips, and was gyrating skillfully, silently, while the younger ones watched. Liza saw Ham's eyes narrow as he too watched Duane. His face was reddening. "Good lord." He turned. "Tom, have you even *noticed* what your daughter is doing?"

Tom opened his eyes. "Umm, yeah," he drawled, reaching down for his half-empty glass of ice tea. "She's got the knack."

"Well, for pete's sake, how can you let her? It's the most lascivious thing I've ever seen. Worse than Lolita!"

Tom laughed. "Sounds to me like you're the one with the problem, Ham. Maybe you should look the other way."

"Ham. It's only a toy," Evvy said.

"Julius, how 'bout it? I bet you'd never let Abby get away with that." Ham turned to Julius, but it was Liza who answered him.

"There'll probably be some weirder fad by the time Abby is ten."

Ham puffed out his cheeks, then let the air out in a blast. He lay back on the blanket he shared with Evvy. A minute later he was up on his elbows. "OK, Tom. You're a lawyer. And Julius. How do you think we can stop this union business at the quarry?" His mouth was a straight and narrow line below the aviator glasses. Sunlight flashed on the glasses as he glared at Tom.

"I don't know what you're talking about." Tom was still drowsy.

"You haven't heard? Our stonecutters, all 300 — most of 'em, anyhow — they've been agitating — night meetings, threatening a picket line. It's killing us, and it's only going to get worse."

"Why shouldn't they have a union?" Julius asked, yawning and stretching his arms over his head.

"It would wipe us out, that's all!" Ham was angry. "They've hired some cheap lousy lawyer. We've gotta stop it. I was counting on you guys for some advice, some help. You know, legally."

"As opposed to illegally, you mean?" Tom was wide awake now.

"Tom! Be nice." Billie patted Desmond against her shoulder.

Liza had seen the quarry once, when Evvy had to take something to Ham's office. Evvy had told her about the accidents — falls from the steep walls of the great pit, men getting caught by the whirling saws and drills that bit into the rock.

"Forget it, Tom. I was dumb to think . . . We have our company lawyers — better than — some bleeding-heart lefty." Ham was on his feet, heading toward their car. Liza expected him to just drive off. Instead, he pulled a carton from the trunk, and walked with it over to where the children were playing.

"OK, kids, what do we have on the Fourth of July?" The children — open-mouthed, bewildered — looked up at him. "Firecrackers, that's what!" he said.

He stuck a red cylinder on the ground, propping it up with a rock.

"Stand back, guys — out of the way, Thurman." Ham struck a match, touched the fuse with his little flame, then scrambled out of the way himself.

Abby cried at the sudden loud noise and came running to Liza. E threw up his hands with a frenzied laugh. Duane put her hands over her ears, then laid one hand on E's trembling shoulder.

"Thurman? Your turn. Here, I'll show you . . ." Ham took a firecracker from the box and handed it to Thurman.

"No." Tom was on his feet. He limped over, and took the firecracker from his son's hand, leading him away. "We're not doing that, Ham. It's against the law here, for one thing."

The two men looked at each other. Tom — lean and pale in T-shirt and jeans, was twisted and seemed to be in pain. Short stocky Ham, dressed in khaki shirt and shorts, looked vaguely military, his grim face half-hidden behind brown lenses. Liza was reminded of General MacArthur making his much-photographed pronouncement, "I shall return." That was how Ham looked. He turned away, toward the tracks. With his matches he set off a string of firecrackers. Pop-pop-pa-pop . . . The sound went on for what seemed like minutes.

"Evvy. E. Time to go." Ham walked back toward the silent group around the table. "Thanks a lot, Billie. The turkey was super, and that sponge cake was a killer. Mind if I take a beer for the road?" He helped himself from the washtub.

Liza and Julius stayed a while longer. No one mentioned Ham or the firecrackers. They helped carry things into the house. Tom stayed in his chair, but he didn't look comfortable.

"Tom, don't you think you should check out that leg with Dr. Blake?" Julius asked.

"I'll see how it is in the morning."

Billie hugged Liza when they were leaving. They didn't usually do that.

"Liza?" It was Billie on the phone next day. "Dr. Blake put Tom in traction. He's home, in bed — for *three weeks*." When Liza hung up, she just stood there, wondering if there were anything she could do that would help.

EVEN AFTER Tom was back on his feet, Liza would some-times run errands for Billie, drive Duane to the orthodon-tist's in Lowell, or pick up some apples at Cox Farm if Billie needed more for her pies. Two afternoons a week Liza had Thurman and Donny over to play with Abby. Some days she would even take Desmond, too, to give Billie a break. Desmond was a plain-looking baby, Liza thought; pale and stiff to hold, plus he kept spitting up his formula.

But every morning Liza let herself into Alice Parlee's house for three silent hours. She was still working her way through the mass of town records the following February when Minx came for one of her visits.

"Come give your old Minx a hug, Abby sweetie," she said on her arrival, crouching down on her toes. The sharp heels of her black sandals stuck out behind her. Abby patted Minx's fur hat, her fur coat.

"Give me a hand, Liza — unh." Minx struggled to her feet. "Your job doesn't seem to have done Abby any harm; she's going to have the family good looks, that's obvious. You're pretty as a yellow daffodil, Abby, what do you think of that?"

Her side of the family, naturally, not mine, thought Liza.

Later, against the rattle of her martini being shaken by Julius, Minx said, "I'm dying to see this spooky old place where you work, Liza. Can you take me there tomorrow? And then I want to see Lolly Clifford, the poor thing."

The next morning Julius took Abby off to nursery school on his way to the train. Liza squeezed oranges and fixed a four-minute egg for Minx.

"Did you warm the egg cup, dearie?" Minx asked, her hands clasped around the cold blue china egg cup.

"That never occurred to me," said Liza slowly. "I guess I always thought the egg would warm it up."

By the time Minx had dressed and put on her orange pancake makeup, Liza was an hour later than usual heading to work, but she decided it was all right for once, considering.

"But this is utterly divine," Minx said when Liza had let them into Alice's house. "It's like something out of — well, you know, one of of those ghastly old novels, *Middlemarch* or something. You won't be working here *forever*, though, will you, dearie? So lonely, absolutely *desperate*."

"Well, people do come in sometimes, for marriage licenses, stuff like that. And actually, the nephew, the one who owns it now, wants to sell the house. So one of these days I'll be moving to an office in the town hall."

"That sounds better. I must say I worry about you, sweetie, turning into an absolute *hermit*." Minx wandered from room to room, her red nails fingering the dusty cut velvet at the windows, stroking the Victorian mahogany chair backs, and straightening blackened gilt-framed oil paintings.

"But I have to finish plowing through all this stuff first. And it's really been fun, believe it or not. Every night Julius wants to hear about all the odd things I've turned up, or the latest scandal. And there've been a few of those."

"I'm longing to hear *all* about it, but now I should go to the Cliffords', if you'll run me up there. Lolly's expecting me. I dread it — poor dear, so hard."

Liza had not been to Le Pigeonnier since last December, more than a year ago. A long time. Before Derek's accident. The house looked the same to Liza, on the outside. But I'm not sure if I'd ever want to go inside, she thought. Or out to the garden. She watched Minx slither across the icy driveway on her pale nyloned legs below the rippling hem of her football-shouldered mink coat. I suppose I should have helped her, mused Liza, but Minx had already reached the door, which opened before her.

Show and Tell

THE MR. & Mrs. Club was making plans to put on a variety show. Chipper Reilly would be the director. "It'll be similar to a TV talent show," he announced at one of the club's monthly pot-luck suppers. "Sort of like Ed Sullivan, with different musical acts and comedy skits."

To Liza's astonishment, Julius agreed to take a part. He was to be the Sheik of Araby.

"That was Chipper," he had told Liza one evening after a long phone conversation. "Tilly Follen is going to do her belly dance, and they needed someone to be the sheik. They all seemed to think I'd be good." He looked away.

Liza put her hand over her mouth, trying not to laugh. But still she was pleased, and oddly proud.

From then on Julius was often out at night, rehearsing. They rushed through dinner, with Liza left to put Abby to bed and do the dishes. Then she had a peaceful hour or two to read or work on her town history.

"Do we have a loin cloth?" Julius asked her one morning.

"A *loin* cloth! No, we don't."

"But that's what I'm supposed to have for the show. That's what sheiks wear. That and a turban."

"Hmm. I've always pictured sheiks dressed in puffy pantaloons. Not that we have any of those around, either."

"Liza, why are you always so literal? Chipper *wants* me in a loin cloth. I have to sit with my knees crossed."

Liza shrugged, not sure what Julius's knees had to do with it. "I guess we could figure out something — an old sheet, do you think? But you'll freeze; the town hall is really cold."

"We all have to make sacrifices," Julius said.

Liza turned to look at him, but he was serious. "I'll sacrifice a sheet," she said.

Julius would come home at night, after rehearsals, humming snatches of old songs. Occasionally he'd let out a short burst of laughter.

"What's so funny?" Liza, already in bed, looked up from her book, her hornrims on her nose.

"Just something that happened. You wouldn't understand."

I bet I would, Liza thought. But she surprised herself by not really caring. A couple of years ago she would have felt left out and miserable.

Julius seemed a bit hurt by Liza's apparent indifference to the big show. "You could come to a rehearsal, you know, see what we're doing."

So Liza drove herself to the dress rehearsal. When she walked in Pearl Swenson was singing from the stage in a tremolo soprano that rebounded from the pressed tin ceiling: "Three coins in the fountain . . ." She kept one hand pressed to the V of her baby-blue décolletage, while the other hand flared out from her hip in a coy theatrical curve. Her forehead glistened.

Liza spotted Evvy and went to join her. Together they sat through a can-can, a patriotic number, and Spider Follen's incomprehensible Scottish monologue. "A little more oomph," Chipper would shout from time to time, waving his cigarette. "Let's have it again."

From a record player came the tinny alien sound of some wailing wind instrument, spiralling, whining. Finally, thought Liza. When the curtain opened there was Julius, sitting cross-legged, pretending to blow on a flute. He was bare-chested, coated in orange makeup, with black eyebrows and a blue towel around his head. Do I know this man? Liza's stomach knotted. She recognized the towel. I didn't know he'd taken that, she thought; it has my initials on it. Their old sheet, or part of it, was looped around his hips; Liza could see a little corner of his striped boxer shorts peeking out.

Then Tilly entered from stage left, draped in veils and glittery bangles.

"So fat without her girdle," whispered Evvy.

But Liza, her heart still pounding, was amazed by the way Tilly could move her stomach up, down, and around, tapping her tambourine in time with her wiggles and the unearthly music. What is Julius thinking? wondered Liza, feeling a lurching knock of jealousy. He's handsome, even in that horrible cloth. All these rehearsals, she thought, suddenly frantic. And Julius, half-naked and inches away from this writhing woman. She tried to recall if he'd seemed different lately. I'm so naïve, she told herself.

Now from a basket beside him — Liza's sewing basket! — Julius pulled a long green snake. He fluttered the snake in front of voluptuous, gyrating Tilly, while the music spiralled louder, faster. Tilly waggled her hips, shook her tambourine, and twirled her stomach right at Julius. The sparkly jewel in her navel twinkled and flashed. Liza shut her eyes; she felt flushed and sick. The men around her whistled and stamped.

"Attaboy, Julius," yelled Skip Shoemaker. The curtain closed to clapping and cheers.

When the lights came on, Liza slumped down, worn out as if she'd been the one doing all that gyrating.

Julius was already up when Liza woke the next morning. He'd left smudges of orange all over the sheets and his pillowcase. Liza burrowed down in bed again, facing away from the ugliness, but caught by the stale sweet smell. She felt sick.

The door opened, and in came Julius and Abby. Julius was carrying a tray with coffee and sweet rolls. Abby, as solemn as if she were in a religious procession, held a glass jar of dandelions and the first tulip from the garden.

Liza sat up. "What's going on? That's pretty, Abby. But why? Look at this mess . . . it *stinks*." Shaking her head, she flapped the sheet. "It'll never come out."

"Uh-oh." Julius made a face. He and Abby looked at each other.

Liza felt all mixed up inside.

"I don't know if I can stand to do this show one more time," Julius said. "You wouldn't believe how awful . . . that fat stomach right in my face. Dripping with sweat, and *vile* perfume. That's what we're still smelling!" He pushed a window up as high as it would go.

When he turned back he made a comic face and waggled his hips. Abby and Liza began to laugh, then they all sat on the messy bed, eating, spilling crumbs.

Liza sipped her coffee. "Well, your fans seemed to like it," she said, after a while.

"It's better from a distance, believe me. Never again!"

"Don't forget Bunny's coming. He wants to see you in the show."

"Aagh. Bunny." Julius put his head in his hands.

"Just think, tomorrow night and it'll all be over. And you know Bunny; he'll get a big charge out of it." Liza put her arms around Julius. She didn't even mind the smell.

THE CHURCH bell began striking noon. Twelve slow bongs. Liza let herself out of Alice Parlee's house, locking the door behind her. Then the strangest thing happened. The station wagon seemed to steer itself up the hill toward Le Pigeonnier, in the opposite direction from home. The car turned into the Cliffords' driveway. Liza pulled out the key. The tolling had stopped and the reverberations died away. She sat there for a minute in the silence.

It was a year and three months since Derek's accident. Except for just turning around in the drive once, Liza had not been back here in all that while. Only in dreams. Now she found herself pulling the rope to ring the doorbell. Only one bong, a brassy note that hung on the air. She waited, then knocked. There were no cars in the driveway; no car in the open door of the carriage house.

When no one answered her ring, Liza walked around the house. The trees were leafing out, pale green silk, and the lawn was dappled with yellow dandelions. She stood by the tennis court: the net was gone; grass and weeds pocked the corners of the clay surface, like a rash that would spread. Dark sodden leaves from last autumn lay clotted behind the rusty roller.

The long straight walk beneath the clipped hornbeams pulled her on. She stepped over the muddy patches. The leafy canopy was just beginning to unfold, shiny new furled green among the silver-gray tracery of the interlaced branches. When she came to the stairs leading up to the tree house, she climbed up, bumping her head on a low branch. A child-size teacup lay in a puddle beneath the little table. Liza turned to go down.

When she reached the gap in the dense hemlock hedge at the end of the path, she walked on through, seeing in her mind the slender shape of Derek sitting on the wooden bench, holding a book. She almost bumped into a grass-covered mound as high as her head, as wide as half the tennis court. The bomb shelter. Of course. She'd heard; still, it was a shock to come upon it, this "shelter," replacing herbs, fruit trees, the raspberry patch, and even, it seemed, Derek himself.

She turned and hurried toward the house. The sun was reflected off the long windows of the big room, the party room. You couldn't see in unless you pressed against the glass. Liza, breathless, couldn't seem to stop herself from peering in, shielding her eyes with cupped hands. The grand piano was near the window; its keys were covered. She saw in the shadows what looked for an instant like a person, seated on a sofa. The shape resolved itself into a pile of pillows, and Liza fled.

In the driveway she was startled by the gardener, standing like a statue, holding a rake in one hand, eyeing her up and down. She'd seen him here before, back when she'd been young and carefree, barely noticing him doggedly pushing a lawnmower back and forth across the grass.

"Oh," she said now. "I was just . . . I'm a . . ."

He interrupted. "They ain't here. Be back tomorrow."

Why did I come here? she asked herself when she was back in the car, her heart still racing. She sped along the roads toward home, toward Abby and Wendell and the comforting bulk of Mrs. Brine the sitter.

THREE YEARS after the celebrated one and only Mr. & Mrs. Club Variety Show, Liza was wheeling a rattly shopping cart out of the Atomic Super Market when she almost ran into Evvy Clifford hurrying in.

"Haven't seen you in a dog's age, Liza. What's up with you guys?"

"Well, my book is finished at last. *Rock Hill: The First Two Hundred Years.* It should be out by Christmas."

"Fabulous. Two hundred years. Actually — I shouldn't say it, but it doesn't sound like my kind of book. But then you've always been the serious type."

Evvy looks different, thought Liza. And it's not just the makeup — even though she never even used to wear *lipstick.* Those pouches under her eyes, and her mouth, so tight-looking when she's not talking.

"We should get together, Evvy. Remember what fun we used to have?"

"Yeah." Evvy sounded dubious.

Liza hesitated. "And how are the Cliffords?"

"She took it really hard — you know, Derek, and then all this other stuff. The old man's away more than ever."

"So what about you, Evvy? Things are really changed, aren't they, now with our kids in school."

"Yeah, a lot of things are different. My life has gone crazy. New York last weekend, then I'm going cruising for a week in March — the Windward Islands — with this guy I just met in Aspen, Pete, I forget his last name. If he ever told me."

Liza stared, trying to make sense of what she was hearing. "And Ham?"

"You haven't heard? I thought everyone knew everything in Rock Hill." She made a face. "He took off a month ago, in *my* station wagon — heading west, he said — with Myrtle Doggins, his father's secretary. He didn't even say goodbye to E."

Liza's knees felt quivery; she saw the desperation in Evvy's pinched face. "I can't believe it."

"Old man Clifford believes it — you should have heard him. Ham will get fed up with Myrtle pretty fast — talk about *dumb*. But his father's already changed his will. Ham has burned his bridges — for good."

"But what about you? And E?" Liza could hear her voice turn shrill.

"The Cliffords will take care of us, never fear. And maybe I'll find me a rich sugar daddy; I'm working on it."

When Liza saw Evvy's chin tremble, she dropped her shoulder bag on top of the groceries and reached out. But Evvy held up her hands, and dashed toward the store.

"Gotta rush," she called over her shoulder. "I'll see you."

Liza sat in her car for three or four minutes before turning the key.

BILLIE RAY Ryan and Liza were sitting in the Adirondack chairs in Liza's garden. Apple blossoms showered like snow onto the grass. Along the stone wall fat peony buds were showing pink. A puff of air shattered the white tulips, setting petals to drop one by one. They'd seen the orange flash of orioles, nesting in the lowest trailing branch of the old elm.

"I can't bear your leaving." Billie shook her head. "Aren't you sad at all?"

"Oh yes, if I think about it. I even got sentimental about the last rhubarb! And Julius has worked so hard on the vegetable garden, fending off woodchucks, digging out rocks . . ." Liza looked toward a bare brown plot with a wavy wire fence around it. "He's started some radishes and lettuce even though we're moving. For the new people, I guess." But Billie was not a gardener.

They could hear Tom's voice, Julius's, and the treble calls of the children, floating in the still air from the pasture where the sheep used to be. They were tossing and kicking a red rubber ball of Abby's in an approximation of soccer. Desmond Ryan, now three, scampered crazily through the field of play. "Outta the way, Desmond," called Thurman. The mothers could hear Duane, sounding like a mother herself: "Watch out, Desmond, honey, you'll get bumped."

"How about all the work you've put into this house, Liza?" Billie had put in work, too, helping Liza hang wallpaper.

"Oh, I know," Liza said, with a shake of her head.

"And what about you, Wendell, moving to the city?" Billie rubbed his head behind his soft ears. She was the only person besides Liza, Julius, and Abby who paid any attention to Wendell.

"I used to think we'd be in Rock Hill forever. But Julius really needs to be closer to the office now that he's finally made partner. And with my new job at Wheelock College, and maybe graduate school . . ."

Billie let her hands fall to her broad lap, a sinking gesture. "I *hate* Rock Hill; I always have." Her hands became fists, beating the wide arms of her chair. "And we'll never leave, I know it." Now her hands were cupped over her face.

Liza didn't know what to say. Guilt stuck like a lump in her throat. "You're what I'll miss most, Billie. But we'll come out to see you; you'll come in. Cambridge isn't *that* far." So many things she couldn't say: the wonderful private school where Abby would go, along with all the professors' bright kids, the square house on Francis Avenue with the columns in front. The Ryans could never afford these things, even if they wanted them.

"I know, I know." Billie shook her head, trying to smile. "But you're really my only friend, you know — in this wasteland." Her big brown eyes filled. She blinked, holding back tears.

"I'll need your advice on decorating. The house is all brown now; some old dean and his wife were there forever. The ceilings are so high we'd never be able to put up wallpaper ourselves, but I'd love it if you'd help me pick out colors and all."

Liza tried without success to picture herself and Billie going through the new house together, deciding on the decor. She loved Billie, but they were too far apart, maybe always had been. And now the gap was widening. For the first time she saw Billie as a tragic figure: wrenched out of West Virginia, roosting briefly in Cambridge as an atypical law school wife, and now settled uncomfortably but probably forever in the narrow-minded Yankee backwater of Rock Hill. I've depended on Billie, Liza thought despairingly, used her, actually. And now? She's my best friend, and I'm abandoning her. She tried to think of something, anything she could offer.

They heard wails coming from the sheep pasture. Desmond Ryan.

"I better go get him, poor baby." But Billie didn't move.

"He'll be OK," Liza said. "Tom's there, and Duane. Are you still thinking about starting an antiques shop? I bet you'd do well; country pieces are getting really popular."

"I already have our garage full of stuff." Billie drained her glass of Pepsi. "But you know, I'd need a place. Tom's actually encouraging me; he's already talked to the selectmen about the old schoolhouse — that'd be about perfect. If it doesn't cost too much."

"I can't think who else would want it," Liza said. With Wendell leading, they walked slowly through fallen petals toward the pasture, their children, and the fathers.

"How about my ties? Make sure they're packed flat; no wrinkles."

Julius and Liza were sitting at the kitchen table over the last dinner in their old house. The movers were coming early the next morning. Liza had been working for days, packing clothes, Abby's toys, her grandmother's porcelain tea caddy, the shell-shaped Steuben ashtray, the Lalique birds that Bunny had given them for their wedding present. Their house had filled up after her father died. More old furniture, old photo albums, her mother's Belgian glasses and Wedgwood china, all precious to Liza. Julius couldn't understand why she didn't just leave it all for the movers to pack.

"They're the pros, Liza, for pete's sake. You're making such a fuss." Julius stabbed the peas on his plate, poked with his fork at the creamed chipped beef. "Why can't we just have a normal dinner, at least?"

"I decided this was a good night to use frozen food. I'm not apologizing." Liza kept on eating.

Julius said nothing. The kitchen felt empty and echo-y with the curtains down. The big plate glass windows were black. It felt strange without Abby; she was spending two nights with the Ryans. Wendell was gone too. Liza had dropped him off at the kennel. Mrs. Barnwell's wasn't actually a kennel; it was just her white house, where big dogs and little dogs hung out of all the windows, barking when you drove up.

"Couldn't you take *one* day off to help with the move?" Liza leaned on her elbows, facing Julius across the table.

"With the Ferguson brief due on Friday? Are you kidding? And besides . . ." He softened, reaching out to pat Liza's arm. "you're much better at this stuff. I'd only be in the way. Actually — if the truth be known — you're better at a lot of things."

The movers had said they'd be there by eight. Julius rushed around that morning, and was giving Liza the usual noisy kiss on the cheek at six-thirty.

"You've never gone to work *this* early," Liza said. She was still in her pink nightgown. "Why today of all days?" She was annoyed, but as soon as he drove out of the driveway she felt glad to have a last hour there, entirely alone. She dressed, stripped their bed, and packed a final suitcase.

In the kitchen she poured the last of the orange juice into a paper cup and looked around. We were so proud of this kitchen, she thought. We felt so avant-garde, with our big windows, and all this Design Research Swedish modern stuff. And now look: those cone-shaped light fixtures are *hideous*; how could we? Probably the new people will make it all quaint and colonial. Liza laughed out loud.

The other rooms pleased her more. Julius's dark green study seemed cozy and, well, familiar. The guest room *was* nice, even though Bunny had always complained of the cold. Minx complained, too, actually. You'd think we could have boosted the thermostat a notch for them, thought Liza. Abby's room — such a little girl's room. She was a baby when we came, and now she's almost through first grade. A corner of the wallpaper had come loose, the paper she and Billie Ray had hung — so long ago, it seemed.

She gazed at the room she and Julius had shared for six years as if it were a model room in a museum. Our bed, she observed, takes up more than half the space. Stripped down to bare ticking, exposing two parallel hollows in the mattress, the bed seemed to her more like a field of battle than a place of rest. She recalled cold feet, Julius's back turned to her like a wall, times when she'd silently cried herself to sleep, times when she'd shut her eyes to remember Derek. And, oh yes, some happy warm times when Julius seemed to appreciate her, when she was reminded of the brilliant, invincible Julius she'd once worshipped. Even the time when his stage make-up got all over the sheets. Now she knew him as just Julius. But he needed her. No one else could understand him as she did. No one else would love him as she did. Aloud she said, "I do love you, Julius. And I need you." She saw something under the bed, and bent to retrieve one of Julius's black socks, balled up and a bit dusty.

She went out for a last look at her garden, still shrouded in a pearly morning mist. The wet grass soaked her blue sneakers. The air was sweet with lilies of the valley. She sniffed a fat pink Sarah Bernhardt peony, a creamy New Dawn rose. The purple irises were about to open. From her shirt pocket she drew the smooth white stone, the stone Derek had given her once, long ago. She rolled the stone in her fingers as she'd done before, imagining it as soft. She chose a mossy spot behind the old crooked apple tree at the end of the garden. Kneeling, she pried back the moss with her fingers, and scooped out a bit of earth to make a nest for the white stone. She covered it over and patted it down. There, she said to the stone. You belong here in Rock Hill. You and Derek. She stood up.

She heard the hiss and whine of truck brakes in front of the house. With wet sneakers and dirty hands she went into the house. She watched the huge red van back into their narrow driveway, brushing pine boughs as it came, snapping off a few.

Three men jumped down. The boss of the crew strode with springy steps to the door where Liza waited. "*Good* morning, ma'am. Alvin from Allied, at your service."